TIMES NOT
TRAVELED

AUTHORED BY:
E G GLOVER

For information address Relative Term Press,
71 CO RD 454, Killen, AL 35645

Cover Art by Stephanie White, Steph's Cover Design
Published by Relative Term Press

ISBN-13: 978-0692203927
ISBN-10: 0692203923

First Relative Term Printing May 2014

Works by E G Glover

The Mystery Hill Series:
A Twist In Time
Times Not Traveled

http://egglover.wix.com/books

All *Mystery Hill Series* titles available on Kindle and paperback from Relative Term Press!

Works by E G Glover
with L R Barrett-Durham

The Fear Series:
Fear the Beast Within
Fear the Thirst Within
Fear the Emptiness Within

http://www.Facebook.com/FearAndTrust

All *Fear Series* titles available on Kindle and paperback from Van Pelt Press!

To my daughter, Annika.

My one true hero!

TIMES resembling chaos, it questions reason.

NOT only the present, but events long past,

TRAVELED blindly in another season.

- E G GLOVER

PROLOGUE

Monday, September 22, 2014, 6:44PM
Autumn Equinox...

Richard Adahy stood at the far north end of the stone circle on top of Mystery Hill and passed his hand through his long windswept hair. He watched the last rays of the sun vanish from view on the horizon. A hollow solemnness pierced the Indian's face as twilight turned to black around him. He surveyed the woodland and took a step toward the circle's center as the wind that twisted through the trees fell into an eerie stillness.

The gasps of a man's labored, raspy breathing interrupted the sudden silence which surrounded him. Richard spun to see a figure standing just outside the stone circle, an arm pointed stiffly in his direction.

A tightly gripped 9mm pistol set locked in the man's shaking hand, his finger nervously resting on its trigger. Sweat rolled from his pores, the collar of his shirt a shade darker than the rest of the fabric.

It took the stranger a moment to catch his breath. His words came out muddled as he stammered, "What...what did you do to her?"

Richard held up one hand in a reassuring gesture. The man's body trembled with panic, likely kindled by the spectacle he had apparently just witnessed.

"Nothing that she didn't wish to happen," Richard replied calmly.

Percy's shrill call resonated off the ancient stones of Mystery Hill and interrupted the men's tense confrontation. Richard's eyes widened with surprise at the presence of his feathered familiar as he dived down, targeting the man in front of him. The stranger's gun fired with a deafening crack. Its sound circulated through the thick air.

Richard lowered his arms. Mystery Hill grew silent once more.

CHAPTER ONE

Friday, September 19, 2014
Three days earlier...

Abby Morris looked up from her computer screen. Her lips formed a slight grin as Thomas Collier walked over the shop's threshold and toward the counter. Her eyes quickly darted back to her monitor as she bit her lip slightly, trying not to appear overly excited by his presence.

She started typing haphazardly on her keyboard when a small rapping on the counter's glass made her jump slightly. Abby looked up into an ocean of blue eyes. She felt her cheeks start to burn when she realized she had been staring at him for a few too many seconds.

His chestnut hair waved across his brow as he spoke, "Excuse me, ma'am. Could you tell me how much it would cost to get you to look at my laptop?"

She took his hand and squeezed it gently, finally breaking her gaze, "What's wrong with it?"

Thom's grip tightened around her hand and a slow smile crept across his face as he replied, "I'm not sure. I think it may have been something I downloaded. Maybe if you look under...my accessories, you might be able to fix it."

She let go of his hand and gave him a playful smack on the arm. Abby leaned her elbows on the counter and offered him her lips, which he quickly took with his.

As he pulled away, he gave her chin a quick caress, "I'll be waiting for you outside."

Looking at her watch, she returned, "I'll be out in five minutes."

Abby covertly watched him as he walked from the electronics shop while the slightest grin flashed across her face, her green eyes locked on his bottom.

∞

Thomas Collier strutted out of *Byte Me* with a smile similar to Abby's etched on his lips. Every time he saw her, he lost his heart to her that much more. Just the slightest touch of her filled him with an electrical charge he couldn't deny.

Thom approached a bench in the mall's main hallway, turned, sat, and combed his hand through his earth-toned, brown hair. He could just make out Abby's shape through the shop's tinted glass as she waited on a customer.

Her constant energy amazed him. It was an unbridled force that none could claim, though he hoped to try. He watched as she buzzed about the shop, helping her customer find the right piece of computer equipment. Thom had to stifle a laugh at seeing the determination she put into her job, her ginger locks waving behind her as she bounced from one store display to the next, making doubly sure the store's patron understood the different PC components. She never let up on what needed to be done.

Thom observed as one of Abby's coworkers took her place behind the counter as she finished up her sales spiel. She gave her customer a firm hand shake, and directed him to the register.

Abby disappeared in the back room for a moment, then emerged with a small purse draping one shoulder, and wearing a smile that he could not help but return as he watched her exit the store. Her green orbs locked onto his face as she sashayed provocatively in his direction. Thom surveyed her intently as she approached. His scrutiny took in her red tresses falling down over her tight-fitting green blouse, his eyes stopping just briefly to admire her curves.

Abby sat herself tightly next to Thom on the bench; her smile turned into a mischievous grin as she noted him admiring her. She placed one hand on his knee and gave it a playful squeeze, "See something you like?"

Thom looked her up and down once more, his eyes stopping at hers, "Uh huh," he answered, his tone infused with a suppressed desire.

She ran her hands through her hair, pushing it behind her ears and leaned toward Thom to greet him with a soft kiss.

Closing his eyes, he took in her fragrance as her touch coursed through his body.

Abby broke the kiss and smacked Thom on the leg, "So, what do you want to do tonight?"

He scratched at his chin a moment, all the time keeping his eyes locked on her gaze, "Hmm…maybe go to the movies? It's been a while since you had an evening off work."

Abby huffed at his words, "Tell me about it! Seems like all that I ever do is work."

Thom laughed at her phony annoyance with her job. She loved what she did, although he never could figure out why. From what he could deduce from seeing her work over the past couple of months, Abby's job mainly consisted of people coming in and quizzing her about how to fix their various computer issues. It differed greatly from his job at *The Gazette* where he spent most of his day staring at other people's words, hours of endless deciphering semi-talented journalist voices into something intelligible. It was a thankless job being an editor, but it paid well.

Abby just crinkled her nose at his laughter as she grabbed his hand and stood, "Come on. I want to get there before all the good seats are taken."

Thom rose to his feet, never breaking her grasp on him. As they walked hand in hand down the mall's long corridor, he could feel happiness swell within him. He was completely bewitched.

Abby broke her grasp on his hand and stole a kiss from his cheek, "I have to run to the restroom before we leave the mall. Be right back." Thom watched her disappear down one of the mall's side corridors.

He stopped at the edge of the food court and felt a slight twinge on the back of his neck and the hairs on his arm rose as if he were being watched by someone. Thom whipped around to see an all too familiar face sitting at one of the tables, nibbling on a french fry. He groaned silently and tried to pretend he hadn't seen her.

It was too late.

"Thomas," the girl's voice reverberated in his ears.

He slowly turned toward her, trying his best to look exasperated at seeing her again. He struggled to find words that conveyed annoyance, yet were softened with the humor they used to enjoy. "Hello, Sarah," was the best his lips could muster, his inner conflict winning out over his wit.

Sarah used her free hand to push her brunette ringlets behind one ear, "Fancy running into you here." Her voice oozed with such thick sarcasm Thom wondered if he should alert the janitor to bring a bucket and mop.

Thom sighed, his voice deep with regret, "Why are you here?"

∞

Abby rummaged through her small bag, removed her favorite green eye shadow, and gazed into the mirror as she touched up the lids of her eyes.

She could not help but smile again at the thought of Thomas. She loved 'foxing' herself up for him. His eyes never left her when she entered a room, and she loved it!

Abby recently moved from Bangor to Manchester after being offered a job at the Mall of New Hampshire, a welcome change that couldn't have come too soon. Her home town limped along at its slow pace, dreary and predictable. She needed something completely new.

When her boss in Bangor told her of the opening at another computer store in Manchester, she jumped at the chance, if only to get away from her overprotective older brother that constantly stayed in her personal business.

Abby smiled at her reflection as she clicked the compact closed and stuffed it back into her bag, "Too hot for *his* own good," she teased as she winked and made kissy faces at the mirror.

A cloud of doubt crept over Abby, but quickly dissipated when someone entered the restroom. She hastily collected her bag and headed for the exit.

∞

Thom adjusted the front of his button-up shirt, his body suddenly cold, "Are you following me…again?"

Sarah smiled slightly as she nibbled on one of the fries from her tray, "I have no reason to follow you. Abby made that quite clear the last time I saw you two out together."

Thom slid his hands in his blue jean pockets, and searched for something to say to his previous lover, "I wish you would just stay away from us. You know it sets Abby off every time she sees you."

Sarah's expression turned from defensive to incredulous as she gaped at Thom in disbelief, "Do you think that I simply follow you around like a little lost puppy since you broke up with me? I have just as much right to be in this mall as you do, you know!"

She rose to her feet, taking her half empty tray in one hand and her purse in the other. She jabbed the food tray and its contents into the trash can, the sound of plastic on metal echoing in his ears.

Thom looked at his feet in embarrassment, trying not to meet Sarah's eyes. She marched straight up to him, caught his chin with her thumb and forefinger, and directed his head so his eyes were level with hers, "I want you to understand something. That girl is bad news!" Thom stammered but Sarah cut him off, "I really don't care what lies you have told yourself, but mark my words, she's trouble, whether you want to see it or not!"

Thom pulled away from Sarah's grasp, her blue eyes flashing with a level of contempt he had never witnessed from anyone.

Sarah twisted on her heels and walked away, leaving Thom to stare once again at his feet. He tried to reconcile the Sarah that he had fallen in love with, to the suspicious and angry woman that she had become.

Thom felt a delicate tap on his shoulder causing him to start as he spun around.

"What's wrong?" Abby questioned as she took a step back.

Thom wiped the thin layer of sweat from his forehead as his heart slowed to a normal rhythm, "Nothing, you just scared me, that's all."

Abby flashed him a look of disbelief, "Are you sure? Did something happen while I was in the restroom?"

Thom caught sight of Abby's lovely eyes and all his troubling thoughts melted away. He took her hands in his and fashioned his best teasing, suggestive smile, "Nothing happened for you to be concerned about, other than your absence pulling oh so hard at my heart," he winked his usual blue flash of muted devilry, "You know you can't leave me alone."

Abby's look of confusion melted away as she petted at his palms. He leaned forward and gave her a loving, yet playful kiss, "Come on. Let's get outta here before we are late for the movie."

Thom wound one hand into hers and led her to the mall exit. His mind battled guilt for ignoring the pull at his heart that at one time filled it, but he knew from experience that Abby would be irate if he enlightened her with the knowledge of Sarah's presence. It was a battle in which he wanted no part, not tonight.

CHAPTER TWO

Sarah Wisdom wiped a single tear from her cheek as she made her way back to Sunset Ridge Apartments. The glare from the oncoming traffic burned her eyes as they began to fill. Home seemed like the best place to be after the night's recent events.

Every sight of Thomas overwhelmed her heart with loss, and it poured out of her in the form of anger, mixed with overwhelming jealousy and spite.

She watched listlessly as rain softly started covering her windshield.

"How fitting," she sighed and reached for her wipers and eliminated the shower from her vision.

Three months had passed since Thom had left her. Abby had been an overpowering force in his life ever since she had moved to the area, even though he had denied it.

Sarah knew their relationship was in trouble from the very first time Thom and she had gone into the mall electronics shop. She was positive that a gaze which had always been reserved for her washed across Thom's face at the sight of Abby.

A tiny spark of hatred toward Abby lit that day, but Sarah didn't voice it. She wrote it off as her overactive imagination. As time passed, the thoughts of Thom's potential affair unceasingly drummed an out of tempo rhythm in her heart. Its beat continued until she could no longer contain it, her jealously finally erupting with little thought of its repercussions. Her words cut deep into Thom's heart, and there was no taking back the bite of her rage. She never had proof of Thom's infidelity, and that was the one thing that burned in her soul. But, either way, he was with Abby now. It was all the proof she needed.

Sarah shattered back into reality as she parked her car in its familiar spot. By this point, the rain shower had turned into a full blown thunderstorm. She wiped her eyes once more, and watched the small shrubs around her apartment building dance in the wind's gale.

Before opening the car door to receive her soggy welcome home, Sarah reached for her keys resting in the ignition and grabbed her purse as she bitterly echoed her earlier statement, "How fitting."

∞

Thom sat in the chilled theatre while the larger-than-life images of Liam Neeson working as an unlicensed private detective filled the screen in front of him. All Thom could concentrate on was the petite hand that rested in his and the woman attached to it. He looked over at Abby, her eyes transfixed on the movie screen, as the film's action flashed against her flushed cheeks.

Gunfire from the film jolted his attention to forward, causing his mind to jump tracks to something less appealing. "What was Sarah doing at the mall? Was she really following him around?" he questioned himself.

At first, all of Sarah's supposedly accidental run-ins with him seemed to be just that, accidental. However, its frequency had grown over the past month, and caused him to think she was truly stalking him. Thom nearly chuckled at the thought of someone being obsessed with his whereabouts. But the more he thought on it, the more sense it made. He squirmed uncomfortably in his chair, the point of the movie in front of him all but lost to his mind's combat.

After nearly a year of being in a relationship with Sarah, she began acting odd, resentful, with little snide comments that made her constant unhappiness known. Thom took a back seat as he witnessed Sarah develop a heightened level of hostility, his every action and reaction analyzed for signs of betrayal. Finally, her paranoia came to the surface. She lashed out at him in a jealous rage that had been completely unexpected, and undeserved. He had always been true to Sarah, though she thought otherwise. She accused Thom of having a relationship with Abby. Her accusation couldn't have been any farther from reality.

Thom washed his hands of Sarah after her outburst, even though his heart reeled from the loss of her affections. He turned cynically away from the love he had believed was his *forever*.

After their split, the news of Thom's single status seemed to circulate around at lightning speed. Something he had attributed to Sarah, although he could never really be certain. Many of his friends had taken it upon themselves to believe he had left Sarah for Abby. Like most assumptions, the facts were lost in the manufactured details as the story was told.

While visiting *Byte Me* to pick up a needed cable for his television, Abby made it quite clear she was interested in him by writing her phone number and a flirty wink on the receipt and planting it inside the bag with his purchase.

Thom looked back down at Abby's hand resting on his knee, and intertwined his fingers with hers. They turned to one another and Abby met him with a single kiss before turning back to the screen. Her kiss set a smile on his face and he turned back to the movie. He became lost in the rush of sensation that hummed in his lips and closed his eyes to relish in the moment.

He blinked his eyes several times as he came to his senses, the movie's credits starting their march up the screen.

Thom looked around, and wondered to himself, "Did I fall asleep?"

Abby turned to him, smiled, and squeezed his hand as a sign she was ready to leave. If he had fallen asleep, apparently Abby had not noticed.

As he led her down the dimly lit hallway of the theatre, he replayed his thoughts from the last couple of hours.

"I hope Abby doesn't ask me about the movie," he thought to himself, "I can't recall a single detail."

As they exited the lobby and crossed the stormy parking lot, he tried desperately to stifle the voice that echoed repeatedly, "Sarah...why won't you stay out of my head?"

∞

Richard Adahy waved as a carload of visitors pulled out of the parking lot in front of his office. He always enjoyed showing off the stone circle to anyone that came to take in its splendor. He always found himself intrigued, if not amused, at their questions about Mystery Hill. Sometimes people would happen upon his place in Salem, New Hampshire purely by accident. Some would tell him they had read an article in a magazine or in a history book. However, in both of those groups, a handful of people would explain to him they felt drawn to the place, and the need to visit there for some unknown purpose. Richard knew why people felt drawn there, though not always the purpose.

He walked toward the door of his office just as a streak of black shot from the sky and landed on his shoulder.

"Caww!"

Stepping through the office door, he gave the crow a couple of rubs on the head. The bird's black eyes shined like a pair of onyx gemstones in the dimly lit room. The crow hopped from the aged Indian's shoulder to land on a perch next to the room's worn wooden desk.

Richard slid into his chair and pulled open one of the desk drawers to produce a container of tobacco. He pulled a pinch of the cherry scented leaves from the small bag and generously filled the bowl of his pipe.

The eyes of the bird never left Richard as he struck a match and placed its glowing tip to the tightly packed leaves. He inhaled a few times, smoke rolling around his face and into the air above him.

Richard waved the match in his hand until the flame was extinguished and turned to face the crow, "Percy, it's been another good day."

The black bird's head bobbed up and down, acknowledging the old Indian's statement.

"I got some work done in my garden, we had a few visitors to the circle," he took a long draw from his pipe, "and you finally managed to catch that old field rat that has been worrying you so."

Percy started cleaning his claws with his beak at the mention of his latest victory.

Richard propped his time-worn boots on his desk and continued to puff on his pipe, the sweet smelling smoke forming a cloud above him.

The crow stopped his cleaning, his attention riveted to the window. His glossy black eyes pointed sharply outside as a heavy gale of wind hit the building, rattling the glass in its frame.

Percy called out in startled excitement and leaped from his perch. He circled the room, his way of informing Richard he wanted out of the office.

Richard nearly fell backward in his chair as he tried to remove his feet from atop the old desk. "What the devil was that?"

Percy flew about the room, cutting paths through the smoke that filled the air.

Richard reached the door just in time for Percy to fly from the office at top speed. Looking outside, he saw the trees sway in a fearful wave toward the direction of the ancient stones at the top of the hill.

Taking his walking stick from its accustomed place next to the office door, Richard made his way up along the old trail, its path leading to the center of the circle.

The wind roared in Richard's ears as it pressed against his back, making the climb up the hill all the more demanding on his old muscles.

As Richard crested the top of the hill he saw Percy circling frantically in the air, the bird's calls barely penetrating the windstorm around him. The feel in the air was not natural, but ominous, and shot fear throughout his entire body. The wind felt as though it were pushing him to the center of the stone ring. He used his walking stick to prevent the swirling air from knocking him to the ground as he passed into the circle. He staggered the last few steps and planted his feet firmly in its center.

Percy orbited above him before landing on his shoulder. A sharp, stinging pain surged down Richard's arm as the crow sank his claws deep into his collarbone.

The trees around them leaned in a clockwise position, the wind blowing at a steady gale around them. Richard lessened his grip on his stick and realized the air at the center of the stones was motionless, stable. He could no longer hear the wind screaming by his ears.

Richard stretched out a hand in front of him to feel the tips of his fingers begin to burn from the wind ripping across them. The pain quickly traveled up to his knuckles and he drew his limb away from the border of the air's rage. He blinked hard at Percy with bewilderment blazing in his eyes.

Night had fallen around them as Richard stood perfectly still within the eye of the windstorm. Other than the sound of his quickening pulse drumming in his ears, all sound around him ceased.

Richard placed a hand over his eyes and began an ancient prayer in the Abenaki language. The words crossed his lips and the soundless void swallowed them. He prayed to Tabaldak to give him the strength and knowledge to understand what was happening around him.

A single beam of light shined down from the heavens and bathed Richard and Percy in a blue light brighter than the sun, though it caused no pain to look into it. He gazed into the brilliance and stretched his arms to the sky. Percy looked up with him, his feathers slicked tightly to his small frame.

After several minutes of silence, a sound penetrated the void around him, a voice unlike anything he had ever heard rumbled, "Awansen."

Richard nodded in recognition of the Abenaki name from his youth and answered in his native tongue, "I hear you!"

The blue light slowly intensified around Richard as he listened to the voice of God within his mind, the sounding voice reminding him of songs chanted around a tribal fire. Tears rolled down his face as the words of the Almighty spoke of his dedication to the Great Circle over the past fifty years. Richard's heart was overwhelmed and lightened by the words that he had done well.

The tears stopped and his face grew somber as he heard the warning of what the future might hold and what he needed to do to prepare for it.

Richard went to his knees, his hands still pointed toward the sky. He felt the blue light pierce through him like an electric shock, and every muscle and tendon in his body tightened and quickly released. Percy jumped from his shoulder as the wash of blue disappeared from the center of the circle.

Richard lowered his arms and cautiously opened his eyes. The soundless void around him was gone and the winds had quieted their gale. The hushed silence was replaced with the usual sounds of crickets chirping in the woods around them.

The perplexed Indian stood slowly and scratched at the back of his head. In all the years he had lived at the foot of Mystery Hill, nothing like that had ever happened.

Richard spun around a few times to survey his surroundings, until Percy caught his eye. The bird stood on a nearby stone, his feathers fluffed from neck to tail. He pecked at the old rock with his long, black beak, and released a quick caw into the air.

Richard smiled at his feathered friend when he met his gaze, "Percy, we've got work to do."

CHAPTER THREE

Saturday, September 20, 2014...

Abby Morris' eyes fluttered at the sound of her morning alarm as she reached over to silence its persistent and repetitive clamoring. She could see the sunlight break in through her bedroom window and quickly rolled back over in protest.

The pillow she tossed over her head did little to mask the light coming through the cracks of the mini-blinds. She groaned and tossed the pillow to the foot of her bed, "Is it morning already?"

With a quick thrust of her legs, she kicked the blankets away and landed on her feet with a slight thud on the floor. Abby stretched her arms high above her head, while releasing a frustrated yawn. Her hands landed in her hair and she tried to run her fingers through the mounds of auburn ringlets that rested on her shoulders, with little success.

She strolled to her dresser and caught a glimpse of her reflection, "My hair looks like a rat's nest!"

She began shedding her pajamas as she walked into the bathroom. Cranking up the water, she stepped into the shower and slightly arched her back as the liquid came in contact with her fair skin. The hot spray soaked her ginger hair, root to tip, as she covered her mane with a conditioning shampoo to help release some of its tension.

While Abby worked at the tangles, she found herself thinking of the wonderful companion she had found.

Thom's memory always seemed to find her in the shower. Abby never thought that moving to New Hampshire would lead to finding such a loving and caring human being. She was so happy to get out of Maine, just to be in a place that no one knew her. Love was the last thing on her mind, but Thom caught her eye the moment they first met.

When Thom came in one day and a co-worker mentioned he was finally single, Abby made her move. After only two months with Thom, she couldn't imagine her life without him next to her. He made her feel complete.

Her one concern, however, was Thom's ex-girlfriend. Sarah always seemed to turn up when they were out together, and it happened a lot.

She hoped that Sarah's constant accidental meetings with them were not some sort of pathetic attempt to get Thom back, and on one occasion, Abby had let her know this in no uncertain terms.

Abby, lost in her thoughts of Thom, was catapulted back into reality by the icy cold water that bombarded her from the shower head. She quickly leaned forward and twisted the facet off, her spine tingling as the last bit of cold liquid hit her back.

She took a towel from the rack next to the shower and wrapped it around her body, then took another to lightly dry her hair, while she sat in front of her mirror.

Abby set down the towel in exchange for a hairdryer and aimed it at her ringlets.

As she gazed into the mirror, she contemplated the good fortune that had manifested into her life...finally.

∞

Richard awoke the next morning to find himself safely in his bed. He was fairly sure he had put himself there the evening before, but his memory was a bit hazy from yesterday's unexpected excitement.

His clock came into view on his nightstand and he thrust the covers from his body. "I've overslept," he announced to the air. He dashed to the closet to grab some clothes for the day and tossed them over his arm.

Richard scrambled toward the bathroom, which was connected to his bedroom, as he tried to wipe the sleep from his eyes. He laid his shirt in a heap on the edge of the sink, and caught a glimpse of one of his hands. The pair of pants he held fell to the floor as he tried to come to terms with what he saw.

Richard took one finger and lightly traced the nonexistent lines that used to cover the back of his hand.

He turned to the mirror and gasped at the reflection that stared back at him. With his thumb and forefinger, he tugged slightly at the tightened skin on his high cheek bone. His hair had darkened to a shade he had long forgotten as he pulled at its length. The lines around his eyes had faded slightly, and cracks along his jawline had turned to simple character lines.

Richard smacked himself in the face, trying to reassure himself he wasn't dreaming, "I've turned young!"

Pulling his shirt over his head, he threw it in the floor and looked at his chest. The muscles in his arms and chest had firmed and the skin over them had grown taut.

Richard clapped his hands together and yelled in glee, "I look thirty years younger!"

Dancing around the bathroom, Richard thanked Tabaldak for his wonderful blessing. He had gone from a man of seventy years to a man of forty overnight.

He stripped out of the rest of his clothes and looked at his younger form in the mirror, an incandescent smile across his lips. All of his old aches and pains had vanished from his body.

Richard leaned forward and touched his toes and sprang back up in delight. All of his old joints had returned to an earlier state of perfection.

Without another thought, he fell to his knees to acknowledge and praise God for the overwhelming reward He had given him. Richard had come from the past to guard the circle as his father had instructed him, and he had done so since nineteen sixty-three. Tears ran down his cheeks as he chanted his prayers of thanksgiving in his native tongue.

After several minutes, Richard stood and wiped his tears, still astonished at the face that stared back at him from the mirror.

His attention pulled away from the reflection and he looked out the small window to see Percy sitting on a tree limb just in view of the Indian. Richard gave his companion a nod and a grin, "Thank you also, my friend."

∞

Sarah sat staring at the end of her kitchen table, a lukewarm cup of coffee in her hand. Running into Thomas last night still had her addled. She had hardly slept the entire night, her brain running over and over again how happy they used to be when they were a couple.

Thomas had always said that she was the one, his soul mate. Sarah had always felt the same way, and told him often. There was a feeling she had around him that was nothing short of magical. She couldn't understand why he would have made such a blatant statement if he never really meant it and how it could have disappeared overnight if he had meant it. It was all Abby's fault.

Sarah placed the rim of her coffee cup to her dry lips and took a slight sip, barely noticing the liquid had lost most of its warmth. She looked around the room, remembering Thom sitting with her on the couch, the two laughing together at various things that seemed so simplistic at the time. They had even discussed marriage, but it was all for naught.

Over the past few months, she had tried to let Thom go, but her heart was not with her. It was still intertwined with his and it hurt in a way that only death could remedy.

Sarah's thoughts turned once again to Abby, and she felt her blood pressure rise inside her, "This was all because of *her.*" Even thinking of the woman's name caused a piercing fury that coursed throughout her entire body. If Abby had never come into the picture, Thom would still be at her side.

Sarah could hear a calming voice inside her mind, whispering to her. She couldn't quite make out the words, but there was definitely a murmuring which was not part of her own thoughts.

Her stare turned from in front of her to the kitchen window, where she could make out a crow sitting on one of the limbs of the massive oak tree outside her apartment. The bird was beautiful, its dark feathers catching the morning light and reflecting it like a black beacon.

The coffee cup echoed as it hit the table, as Sarah slammed it down and headed to her bedroom to get dressed. Her thoughts sounded absolutely insane as she ran her options through her head. As she grabbed up some clean clothes from her dresser, the results from her morning contemplations were quite clear; she wasn't ready to give up the one true thing her heart had ever felt. That meant it was time for action.

∞

The amount of traffic was unfathomable as Thom made his way to work. He had never witnessed this many cars on such a small stretch of road in his whole life. Thom's boss had already warned him of his tardiness just a week earlier. He couldn't afford to be late…again.

He knew a warm welcome was not forthcoming as he parked his blue Honda Accord in front of *The Gazette* building, and quickly slid out of the driver's seat; his eyes focused on the front door as a knot of dread lodged itself in the pit of his stomach.

Thom removed his identification badge from his collar that served as a key to enter the building. With one quick motion he swiped it through the small slot next to the glass door in front of him. A small red light blinked its disapproval. He groaned, swiped the card again, and received the same response.

After the third try, Thom thrust his fist into the door, "Dammit!"

The glass door rattled in its frame which brought an older gentleman from the inside to stand staring at him, a frown etched on his wary face. The security-blue uniform reflected in the window as he spoke, "You can't come in. Mike told me to tell you he'd call you this afternoon."

Thom saw his own mirrored image go pale as he felt the blood drain from his face, "But, Rick..." were the only words he could muster at being denied inside.

The guard crossed his arms over his chest, "I'm sorry, Thom. He said you'd been late way too many times. Maybe you can work something out with him."

Thom lowered his head as he spun on his heels and returned to his car, his anger silently brewing within him.

The car's chassis echoed with his rage as he slammed the door closed, "That asshole! I can't believe he fired me!"

He rested his head on the steering wheel, trying to quiet the fury that swelled inside him, "What am I going to do now? I've been with *The Gazette* for years," he contemplated as his anger was replaced with dread. The thoughts of next month's bills filed and re-filed themselves in his mind.

Thom turned the key slowly in the ignition as he raised his head and realized his next dilemma, "What am I going to tell Abby?"

∞

The monitor's text flickered rhythmically in front of Abby's eyes as she read up on some of the latest computer specs being unveiled within the company in the coming months. She tapped a pen on the counter, feeling a bit annoyed at some of the changes *Byte Me* had decided to test out on their employees.

She pressed the Enter key to continue to the next page, releasing an exasperated sigh, "In a year, they'll change all this again."

The phone in Abby's pocket throbbed against her leg, breaking her concentration on her reading. It was a welcomed interruption when she read the name on the phone's small screen.

"Hey baby, what's up?"

There was an eerie silence before Thom finally spoke, "Would you mind some company this morning?"

Abby placed her pen on her keyboard, concern overtaking her, "Why? What's wrong, sweetie?" She could tell by his tone that something was off.

"I'll tell you about it when I get there. I'm pulling into the mall parking lot now."

"Well, sure. There's not been many customers this morning. We should have time to talk. You sure you're okay?"

"I'm fine," then more silence.

"Okay baby, I'll see you in a few minutes then," Abby's voice shadowed her worry over Thom's odd tenor. "I love you," she added but the line went silent.

Abby looked at her phone and saw the Call Ended message flash across the screen. She slid the phone back in her pocket as she looked out the large plate glass of the shop and into the mall's large hallway.

It wasn't like Thom to be so impassive on the phone. He was usually teasing and upbeat when he called.

She closed the file on the computer she had been reading and looked at her watch. That's when it dawned on her, "Thom should be at work right now," she muttered softly.

Thom passed across Abby's view and entered the shop, his face hard as stone. Abby rounded the counter to greet him.

He grabbed her up tightly and squeezed her in a way he'd never done before. She returned his embrace, which lasted for at least a minute.

Abby felt his arms relax and she pulled away just far enough to look at his face, his eyes filled with shame and remorse, "Baby, what's happened?"

Thom looked at his feet, "I...I lost my job today."

Abby placed her hand on his shoulder, "Oh, Thom, I'm sorry." She watched as he ran his hands through his hair.

"It's my own fault. I was late again. They locked me out of the building," he sighed in frustration.

Abby tried to catch Thom's eyes as two people walked into the store. She smiled at the customers, "I'll be right with you." Her attention turned back to Thom, "Sweetie, go home. I'll come see you when I get off work. We'll figure something out."

Thom flashed a halfhearted smile her way, "I hope." He walked from the store, his shoulder's slightly slumped as he disappeared from Abby's view.

∞

Sarah held her cell phone between her shoulder and cheek as she steered her car onto Interstate 95.

The phone's tone purred softly until a familiar male voice broke in on the line, "Manchester Animal Clinic, how may I help you?"

"Jesse, it's Sarah. I need to call in a big favor from you."

Jesse sighed teasingly, "I don't know. I think I'm all out of favors this week."

"I'm serious! I have to go out of town for a few days and I need you to cover my shifts for me."

"It's no problem. You covered for me last month when I had to visit my grandmother. Is everything okay?"

Sarah tried to think of an excuse to give her co-worker that wouldn't sound as insane as the truth, "I have to go check on a...friend. I shouldn't be gone more than a couple of days, three at the most."

"Sure, Sarah, whatever you need."

"Don't forget that Mrs. Southern is bringing in her cat Momo."

Jesse groaned, "Not that beast. You owe me big for this one," his tone returning back to its usual playful sarcasm.

Sarah chuckled, "I'm sure you will be able to handle her...and her cat too."

She heard him scoff on the other end of the phone, "Maybe."

"Thanks Jesse! I owe you big time."

Sarah let the phone slide from her ear and onto her lap, ending the call with a press of her thumb.

It hadn't been hard to find Abby's previous address, especially since the girl seemed to live online. Sarah had even managed to find photos of her old house.

Sarah's grip on the steering wheel tightened, "People really shouldn't geo-tag pictures of their houses," she mumbled to herself.

Bangor, Maine was only three and a half hours away. It would be midday by the time she arrived. With any luck, it wouldn't take her long to find out...something. Something to prove to Thom that Abby was not what she let others perceive.

To Sarah, Abby felt sinister, but she realized it was going to take something significant to convince Thom to stay away from his new ginger-haired lover.

She shook her head, hoping to suppress her doubt. However, the voice that spoke within her thoughts continued to encourage her more, to carry on her current course of action.

Sarah looked up just as her car started under the next overpass. A large black crow sat on the concrete looking down on her, its wings spread wide, as an unearthly chill coursed down her spine.

CHAPTER FOUR

Thom sat in his apartment, his shame at losing his job still bubbling in his stomach. He had seen this coming and he was mentally kicking himself for his stupidity.

The television whispered slightly in the corner of the room with an endless chatter that never made it to Thom's ears. All he could hear was the rumble in his brain about what he was going to do for money.

A loud rapping echoed from the door; his head turned quickly toward the interruption to his numb silence.

Thom rose to his feet to unlatch the lock and turned the knob. Abby stood there soundlessly as she looked him up and down. Her face had concern carved into it; her eyes mirroring his disquiet and worry.

Abby stepped in and extended her arms forward to give Thom a tight hug. Her hair brushed and settled against his cheek. The smell of her red ringlets intoxicated him, and the rumbling rage toward himself began to diminish until it was washed away with her embrace.

Abby broke the embrace and looked into Thom's eyes, "What happened?"

Thom motioned her toward the couch and waited for her to sit before settling at her side. He rubbed at his temples with one hand before answering, "Exactly what you have already deduced."

Abby tried to catch his eyes with hers as he stared at the floor, but he refused to look upward. She placed her hand on his knee and tried to comfort him by rubbing her hand in a circular motion, "You were late again?"

He finally met her eyes with a slight resentment patterned into his face, "Yes, I was late…again."

Thom placed his hand on top of hers and let out a long sigh, "I don't know what has been up with me recently. I haven't been able to sleep in weeks. I keep having these horrible dreams. Dreams that I am lost," he tightened his grip on her hand and continued, "wandering in the dark."

Abby watched his face, but said nothing.

"It's like I'm looking for something. I'm scrabbling through a thick fog, my arms stretched in front of me, trying to find anything that is familiar."

Thom paused for a moment, debating on sharing the rest of the dream. His cheeks burned with the embarrassment of hearing his nightmare out loud.

Abby slid her hand out from under his and entwined their fingers, "What happens next?"

Thom closed his eyes and spoke, "Then...nothing. I wake up terrified, covered in sweat. I can't go back to sleep afterward, so I just lie there for hours trying to calm my nerves."

Abby looked at him with a glimmer of disbelief in her gaze, "That's all, nothing else?"

Thom stammered for a moment, "You would just have to experience the dream to understand. It scares the hell out of me!"

She smiled at him comfortingly, "Oh, I don't doubt the nightmares freak you out. They would do the same to me."

Thom sensed Abby didn't believe just how terrified the dreams made him. He'd been having them for over a month, almost every night. A full night's sleep had become a distant memory and no rest had finally cost him his job.

The tension in the room got thicker with each second that passed, so Thom moved the conversation away from his dream, "But, my boss is supposed to call me so we can discuss the situation," he managed a half smile, "So maybe I can get this all worked out."

Abby's silence was beginning to drive Thom mad. She just kept looking at him with deep concern.

"Well, say something," he half joked.

"I don't really know what to say. I just want you to know that I am here for you, no matter what happens."

Thom watched as Abby's face lit up with devotion as her words passed over her lips. His grief about the whole situation began to loosen its grip on his heart. He just knew that she would leave him over him losing his job, and over something as useless as him not sleeping. But, even with knowing that, he still could not tell her his entire nightmare. It was simply too embarrassing to admit out loud, even to himself.

Every time he played the dream through his head, it made him almost sick with fear. The details changed just slightly each time, but there was always one thing that remained the same, the large black bird which flew above him. It squawked constantly as he tried to find his way in the darkness before landing just in front of him, its eyes shining like two black mirrors.

Then, there was Sarah. She was always there in the dark. He could hear her voice in the distance, calling his name. The sound of fear was thick in her voice as she pleaded for someone to help her find her way in the hellish darkness that enveloped everything.

Thom had seen Abby's reaction to mention of Sarah before; there was no way he could tell Abby about Sarah being in the dream. Thom rubbed at his forehead again, trying to gauge Abby's reaction to their conversation.

His mind went back to the crow and the black flame in its dark orbs. Thom had no clue what the dreams meant, but his nightly visitor had warped his already misshapen reality.

∞

After kissing Thom goodbye, the door closed slowly behind Abby as she left his apartment. She stood on the small front porch, staring blankly in the direction of her car.

She hadn't known about Thom's nightmares, and the news caused a knot to form in her stomach. Dreams weren't something she took to heart, but the fact his dreams had him wandering lost in the dark was a little too familiar.

For several weeks Abby's sleep had been plagued by an unearthly blackness, a near-blind experience filled only by an ominous voice warning her to turn back. She would reach into the nothingness around her, her arms stretched as far as she could possibly reach.

Occasionally, she heard the sound of a rhythmic flapping, like the wings of a bird, come close to her, and then pass away in the distance only to return again. She could feel the texture of feathers graze by her outstretched arms as she struggled to locate the source of her torment.

The winged strokes would return one last time, louder and labored, coming straight toward her. She could feel the drafts of air near her face as the terrifying shrill of a bird filled her ears before the unseen creature collided into her eyes.

Abby snapped back into reality, still staring in the direction of her car.

She took a deep, steadying breath as she stepped from the porch and positioned herself in the driver's seat. As she placed the key in the ignition and turned it sharply, she whispered firmly to herself, "It's only a dream."

∞

Sarah's car glided along the highway as she passed the sign that marked Bangor's city limits. The brisk Maine air tugged at her steering wheel slightly while she looked for a place to pull off the road.

She stopped at a gas station and took her cell from its resting place on the passenger seat. With the touch of a few buttons, she accessed the phone's GPS.

Her eyes burned slightly from the few hours of driving, her fingers missing some of the keys as she tried to type in a search for the nearest library. Several weeks of sleepless nights had taken their toll on her concentration. A map popped up on the touch screen while she yawned slightly and eyed the front of the convenience store.

Sarah sat her cell phone down as she opened the car door, "I think some caffeine is in order," she sighed.

A bell chimed as she stepped in through the glass door. A tall, thin man nodded to her from behind a newspaper. "Hello," was his only response.

She nodded back before spotting the coffee pot on a nearby counter and picked it up to find just a thin line of black liquid at the bottom.

The guy looked up from his paper again and sighed, slightly irritated, "Hang on; I'll make you some more."

Sarah placed the pot back on the coffee maker's eye and waited patiently as the clerk put more ground coffee into a filter and turned on the machine.

As he cleaned up around the pot, she decided now was as good a time as any to speak, "Do you know where the nearest library is?"

He tossed some stray straw paper into a trash can as he spoke, "There are a couple of libraries near here."

Sarah could smell the coffee brewing, making her eyes open just a bit wider, "I'm looking for somewhere that might have some local news records from several years ago."

The man scoffed slightly, "What are you, a reporter?"

Sarah smiled at the idea of him thinking she was doing some sort of research for a newspaper, "Uh, yes. I'm looking for some information on a person that used to live in this area," she half-lied.

The coffee machine shut off with a slight click as the guy replied, "I would try the library at Eastern Maine Community College. They have a newspaper archive that has a lot of local information in it. Who are you looking for?"

Sarah paused at his question and then reached for the coffee pot to pour herself a cup; a fake smile grew on her face, "It's probably best that I didn't say."

The man shrugged his shoulders as he returned to his spot behind the counter, "Suit yourself," was his only comment.

Sarah poured some sugar and creamer in her cup and gave it a quick stir before going to the counter to pay for the coffee, "Thanks for your help," she added.

The guy totaled up the order and took her money, "No problem. Just keep going on this road. You will see the signs telling you where to turn for the college."

Sarah nodded again and noticed his name tag read 'Carl' as she exited the door. She pressed her nose close to the lid of her cup and took in the aroma of the steam that leaked from its opening, "Thanks for the coffee, Carl."

∞

A cloud crossed over the sun as Richard placed his pipe in its cradle and peered out the window of his office. He was still trying to get used to his rejuvenated body. His ability to see things at great distances appeared to have doubled as he watched Percy fly erratically around Mystery Hill. His call was one of warning, as if something dangerous was nearby.

Richard collected his pipe and exited his office, hoping to see what had his feathered companion so perturbed.

The new swiftness in his steps caught him off guard as Richard made his way down the steps of the porch and onto the path toward the stone circle. As he topped the ancient trail, he saw Percy weave through the air. The bird's attention was focused on the stones at the heart of the mysterious time gate.

Richard stopped and surveyed the sky once more as he called to his companion, "Percy! What is it?"

The bird flew toward him, acting as though he were about to land on the Indian's shoulder, but quickly banked away and headed back to his earlier place. Percy's call still carried a shriek of alarm as he cut above the old stones.

Richard continued toward the center, worry washing over him as he stepped into the ring of stones, "What's gotten into you old friend?"

He watched as Percy would hover slightly and dive sharply at the ground, only to rise up again and circle in the air. After a few more steps, Richard could see and hear the reason for the crow's distress. About twenty feet away, the largest Timber rattlesnake that Richard had ever seen sat coiled directly in the center of Mystery Hill.

Richard froze, his pulse quickening at the sight of the massive reptile. He gaped in astonishment as he judged the snake's length at thirty feet and its girth the size of a man's arm.

He yelled at Percy to leave it be, but the bird ignored him and continued trying to attack his quarry. The animal's thick head rose and fell, its brown cross-bands clearly visible across its scaly surface. Richard knew the snake had to be removed or it would kill his companion.

The reptile raised its mammoth triangular head once more and looked directly at Richard. Its fiendish gaze penetrated deep into the man's soul as the creature's tongue tasted the air with a lazy contempt.

Turning on his heels, Richard sprinted back to his office to retrieve a rifle, his pipe falling to the ground as he ran. He knew that it was illegal to kill a rattlesnake, and he hated to take a life, but it was either the snake or Percy.

Richard grabbed his weapon and bolted from the office door, the rifle loaded and ready as he double-timed it up the path. His pulse quickened with each step as he hurried up the trail.

When he crested the hill, he scanned the sky for Percy. He was nowhere to be seen. He prayed he wasn't too late.

He arrived back at the circle's edge, his weapon raised with his eye positioned on its sites. Richard blinked once, his rifle steadily looking for its target. Richard blinked again and slowly lowered the gun.

He twisted to his left and right as he tried to locate the snake. The creature was gone.

Resting his weight on the rifle, Richard looked once more for Percy. In the distance, a small black speck slowly grew into the shape of his companion. The crow circled him once and landed on his usual place atop Richard's shoulder.

Richard looked Percy over as he petted his head, checking to see if the snake had managed to strike him, but he was uninjured. He looked into the bird's eyes and questioned his friend, "Did you get rid of the snake?"

Percy didn't respond and began cleaning his feathers. Richard's blood turned to ice at Percy's response, or lack of one, understanding that he had done nothing to their unwanted visitor. It had simply vanished.

Richard made a few rounds about the stone circle with Percy still perched on his shoulder. He refused to take chances with his companion. He had to be sure the snake was actually gone. But there was nothing.

He quizzed his feathered friend once more as he retrieved his discarded pipe from the ground, "Was it an omen?" Percy nodded his head reluctantly and continued cleaning his wings.

CHAPTER FIVE

The smell of paper and ink wafted into Sarah's nose as the door to the library gently closed. She'd not set foot in a library in years. Most of her reading came from the dozens of e-books she had bought for her tablet that Thom had gotten her. It was much more convenient than hauling around a large book collection in her bag and served a dual purpose as a laptop. Still, she had not forgotten the intoxicating aroma of the printed word.

A lady sat behind the checkout counter and smiled slightly as Sarah approached, "Can I help you find something?"

Sarah returned the smile and stifled a laugh as she contemplated how to word her request. She drummed her fingers lightly on the counter as she spoke, "I was told that you have a good archive of local news and history."

"We do. Our database is pretty extensive. Come over here and I'll get you set up."

The librarian ushered Sarah to a computer terminal, leaned over the keyboard, and logged into the college's mainframe. She smiled at Sarah and motioned her to take a seat, "Are you a student here?"

Sarah wasn't sure if she should tell her the truth on the matter, worried she might not be allowed to use the college database, "Umm, no. I'm here to do some research, anything pertaining to local criminal acts in the last twenty years."

The young lady hit a few more buttons on the computer and stepped back, "There you go. I've logged you in as a visitor. That will give you two hours' worth of research time."

Sarah replied with a half-smile, "Thanks."

"No problem. If you need anything, just let me know."

Sarah nodded as the girl made her way back to her desk to help another visitor waiting at the counter.

"Two hours," Sarah mumbled, "What am I going to be able to find out in two hours?"

Her eyes blurred slightly and she shook her head to clear her vision as she tried to focus her attention on the computer screen. Her fingers began to work at the keyboard. Sarah typed the first thought that came to mind: *Abby Morris.*

The computer replied with an unsatisfactory: *No results found.* The blinking cursor seemed to mock her with its steady rhythm as she tried to broaden her inquiry: *Local criminal acts from 2004 to present day.*

The screen flashed and was flooded by lists of information that caused Sarah to lean back in her seat. Doubt and frustration beat against Sarah's brain as it quickly became apparent this task would be harder than looking for a needle in a hay stack.

She sighed and looked out the window that was positioned next to her chair. The small opening looked out onto the campus. A timeworn tree stood somewhat cockeyed near the wall of the brick building nearest her, and she could just make out a crow sitting on one of its gnarled branches.

The bird's head bobbed up and down as it prepared to take flight. Sarah watched as the creature disappeared from view into the ash colored sky. She turned her attention back to the computer and sighed again, "This is going to take a lot longer than two hours."

∞

Smoke circled around Richard's office as he puffed silently on his favorite pipe. The cherry flavored tobacco always had a calming effect on his nerves when things troubled him. He rubbed at his chin as he pondered the day's events, his fingers still not accustomed to the revitalized flesh under them.

Percy had not returned to the office after the incident with the rattlesnake. He rarely left Richard's sight, but he had been gone for hours now. The smoke from his pipe thickened as he stepped toward the window, his eyes skimming across the sky. He watched while the sun slowly sank behind a row of trees, worry gradually etching deeper into his brow.

Richard stepped outside to the porch. The wooden boards creaked slightly under his weight. He removed the pipe from his mouth, took in a lengthy lungful of the late summer air, and let it escape slowly from his nose as he tried to remove the concern that brewed in his heart.

The light around him slowly seeped away into night as Richard took one more draw from his pipe. He then tapped the remaining burnt tobacco from its bowl on the heel of his worn boot. His eyelids slid closed as he raised his head toward the sky and whispered, "God, please prepare me for what is to come."

∞

Sarah swung the door closed to the motel room she had purchased for the night. Her frustration leaked from every pore as she tossed her bag onto the bed. Not only was she exasperated from her fruitless research attempt at the library, but she was also filled with shame at driving hours away to dig up filth on her ex's lover.

She ran her hand through her brunette locks as she collapsed on the bed, knocking her bag to the floor. A sigh of irritation echoed through the small room as she kicked off her shoes, their soles hitting the ancient carpet with a padded thud. She laced her toes into the top of one sock and then the other, and slid them away from her feet. The bed sheet's musty odor filled her nostrils as it settled over her still-clothed body.

Sarah rested her arms over her face as she tried to keep the tears of frustration from overtaking her. Flipping over, she buried her face in the stale smelling pillow and felt a single tear leak from her eye and dissipate into the padding below.

She missed Thom more than she had ever dreamed possible. It was like mourning the death of a close friend or family member, but worse, because at least they hadn't *chosen* to leave.

Sarah rested her head on the edge of the pillow and silently cried herself to sleep.

∞

Sarah found herself surrounded by a thick grey fog. Her skin felt damp from the moisture-filled air as she tried to focus her eyes onto anything familiar. The ground squished, soft underneath her bare feet. The mud formed a perfect mold of her toes. Her body was draped with her favorite black nightgown, something that she hadn't worn in months. It had been a birthday present from Thom. Sorrow stabbed at her heart as memories of Thom's face when she'd worn it assaulted her.

Sarah could make out the slightest sound in the distance. It was the sound of chimes. The sound warmed her sorrow. They sounded like the ones that used to hang from her grandmother's porch when she was a child. The rhythmic bells comforted her from the enveloping damp darkness that had shrouded her body. She closed her eyes and lost herself in the happy memories of days long since burned away by time.

Eyes still closed, Sarah ambled cautiously forward, her hands outstretched toward the inviting sound just ahead. She didn't dare open her eyes for fear of losing the thoughts of sitting on the swing with her grandmother, the old woman's smile bringing more comfort as she pressed on through the moist earth underfoot.

The chimes grew louder still, as if they were only a few feet away. If she could just reach them, she would be safe.

Sarah could hear the laughter in her now-departed grandmother's voice, "Come on Sarah, you are nearly here. Just open your eyes."

Not wanting to lose her precious grandmother again, she slowly untightened one eyelid and hoped the old lady would be sitting in her swing as it swayed back and forth. Instead, she found herself still in the dense fog, a large, grey stone sitting firmly in the ground next to her. The ground below her feet had gone from soft earth to stone, so worn that it was obvious it had been put in place in an age long past.

Sarah could just make out movement to her right as she opened her other eye. She slowly spun around, trying to take in what little she could see. The air was still too thick to see very far into the distance, except for the movement that was now in front of where she stood.

"Come this way," the voice cajoled.

Sarah felt anger begin to burn inside her chest. She knew her gran was dead, and the thought of someone...or something stealing a voice so intimate infuriated her.

She sucked in a deep breath as she tried to build up her courage, "I don't know who you are, but this isn't funny!"

The voice returned, "Don't be afraid, Sarah. Come toward my voice."

Sarah huffed; she felt her cheeks burn as her anger rose to her face. She clamped her fists tightly and stormed toward the movement she could see in the murkiness. The movement took shape as she moved forward. A large stone formed in her vision and her eyes were drawn to the top of its mossy surface.

Sarah was only a few feet from the large rock when her toe caught on one of the steppingstones, which sent her to the ground in an undignified heap.

Her cheek rested painfully on the stone floor as she tried to shove herself from the ground. She pushed up with her palms and a gleaming pair of black eyes met hers, her granny's voice shrieking from the opened beak of the dark, winged shape that stood just a few inches away.

"Sarah! Come to me, Sarah!"

Sarah felt her head slump to the ground and abruptly bolted awake, her clothing wringing with sweat. The bed sheet felt murky, dirty. She kicked her feet back and forth until the covering landed in a pile at the foot of the bed.

The bedside lamp blinded her slightly as she switched it on and looked at her feet. Mud covered her heels and caked in-between her toes.

Sarah could still hear the sound of her grandmother's voice echoing in her head, dampened only slightly by the rhythm of her own breathing as she tried to stop her heart from beating out of her chest.

∞

Abby looked up into Thom's eyes as she felt herself go, her body tightening around his as he leaned in and kissed away her breathless cries. His eyes shined with a look of happy accomplishment as he gradually rolled away from her only to snuggle his face next to her neck. His breath whispered across her skin which sent spasms once more through her body.

She ran her nails through Thom's hair, stopping occasionally to gently kiss the top of his head. Her body purred with satisfaction. Thom raised his head to give her a lingering kiss and then settled back into his place.

Her red ringlets lay askew over her feather pillow. She retrieved a strand and began running it along the edge of his ear, "You never cease to amaze me," she whispered across her breath-dried lips.

Thom didn't speak, he simply sighed his approval.

Abby rolled onto her side for Thom to spoon up to her. She faced her window, giving her a view of the tree line illuminated by a neighboring streetlight. Her eyelids tried to bat away the object perched on the nearest limb, a mere ten feet away. The black bird looked toward her and she squeezed her eyes tightly closed. In her mind, she demanded the dark abomination to go away, wishing it from her sight.

Abby reluctantly opened one eye to find the crow absent from its resting place. Quickly shifting in her bed, she looked at Thom who was already fast asleep. She wrapped her arms around him tightly and delicately breathed into his ear, "Please, don't ever leave me, Thom. I love you so much. I couldn't be without you."

CHAPTER SIX

Sunday, September 21, 2014...

Sarah wiped the sleep from her eyes as she entered the Eastern Maine Community College Library. Her restless night had left her feeling blurry and her face reflected that lack of rest as she approached the checkout counter. The same girl from yesterday greeted her with a smile which Sarah did not return, "Here to do some research?"

Sarah nodded, her posture conveying her irritation to the woman's query. "Yeah," was her only reply as she ran her hand through her hair that was still not up to its usual impressiveness due to getting dressed in such a hurried fashion.

The young girl escorted her to a different computer station and logged Sarah in, "You have two hours to use it, just like yesterday."

Sarah huffed, "Is there any way I can get an extension on that? Two hours really isn't enough time for what I need to research."

The lady looked at her with sympathy but sternly replied, "Since you aren't a student here, two hours is all that we can allow. But, I will talk to one of the library administrators and see what I can do."

Sarah halfheartedly nodded and the girl returned to her desk. She was fairly certain there would be no time extension, but she didn't think it would hurt to ask.

She wiggled in her seat slightly and cracked her knuckles as she readied her fingers at the keyboard. Last night's dream tumbled in her brain, but she stubbornly determined to put the nightmare aside so she could concentrate on her whole reason for coming to Maine.

While she painstakingly dug through the library's database, a shadow appeared across her computer screen which caused her to pause. She felt a presence behind her and started to turn to see who had crossed into her personal space when a whisper shot over her right shoulder, "Found any good gossip to report?"

Sarah nearly fell from her chair as she spun around to find the source of the voice. A familiar, half grinning smile greeted her as she repositioned herself. She scolded him in the loudest voice appropriate for their surroundings, "Carl! You scared the hell out of me! What are you doing here?"

The gas station attendant shrugged and motioned his head toward a nearby table, his jet-black hair falling into his eyes, "Ha! I see you remember me. I'm studying...and doing a little research of my own."

"You go to college here?"

Carl brushed his hair out of his face and scowled slightly, "What, you think a convenience store employee can't go to college?"

Sarah felt her embarrassment burn within her cheeks, "No, it's not..."

He tapped her on the shoulder and his dark look was quickly replaced with a toothy grin, "I'm just messing with you. I started here back in the fall. That's how I knew the college was a good resource for local information. What's your name?"

She offered him a guarded smile, "Sarah."

"Well Sarah, it's a pleasure to meet you...again. Have you managed to find any information on the person you've been looking for?"

Sarah was surprised Carl had remembered their conversation at the gas station the day before. He apparently had been more observant during their first meeting than she had realized. She let the heavy frustration roll from her lips as she answered his question, "I've not managed to find anything. But, since I'm not a student here, I can only use the computers for two hours a day."

Carl motioned Sarah's attention back to the monitor as he leaned over her shoulder. He quickly typed his name and user identification number into the awaiting fields.

Name: Carl Spencer
ID# 423219754

He gave the ENTER key a final tap and stood up straight next to Sarah, "There. That should give you access for the rest of the day. Just don't try to hack into any government files or look up any porn. I don't want to get kicked out of school my first year."

Sarah looked up at him, his dark eyes shining with spirited humor. She replied with a smile, "Thank you, but...why are you helping me?"

Carl half-turned back to his place at the table, "Why not? If you need anything else, I'll be right over there."

Sarah nodded and turned toward the monitor before Carl caught sight of her triumphant grin, "Wonders never cease."

∞

Thom looked at himself in Abby's mirror as he straightened the buckle on his belt. The deepening circles under his eyes mocked him. He had lain awake half the night next to Abby's softly snoring form. Yesterday's short conversation with his former boss had gone exactly as he had expected. He wasn't getting his job back any time soon, and it would be in his best interests to look elsewhere.

But losing his job wasn't his only concern. Once again his nightmares haunted him, their ever-repeating loop increasing in intensity. Something in his gut was telling him his life over the past few months had gotten off track.

Thom turned to Abby last night hoping to find comfort in her arms, maybe even an ounce of solace in her touch. It hadn't come; all he found were more worries and worsening nightmares. His feelings for Abby were so tainted with haunting thoughts of Sarah. They drummed a constant cadence in his brain

He stood silently over Abby and watched her as she slept. Her beautiful ginger ringlets lay crisscrossed over her closed eyelids. He thought about wakening her with a kiss but some inarticulate feeling told him not to.

Thom quietly slid on his shirt and shoes before slipping out of Abby's bedroom. He knew he would catch hell for leaving without telling her, but right now, he needed to get away and think without being blinded by the beauty of his gorgeous girlfriend.

As Thom pulled the front door to Abby's apartment closed, he watched as a solitary crow crossed the sky above him. Anxious dread engulfed him. It was time for a little soul searching.

∞

A suppressed growl of barely contained irritation echoed from Sarah's corner of the library. Carl looked up from his pile of books, his eyes filled with concern. He pushed away from the table and walked over to rest his hand on the back of her chair, "What's the trouble?"

Sarah took in a long breath and sighed, "I'm not finding anything on the subject I'm researching. This trip up here was a gigantic waste of time."

Carl rolled a chair next to hers and propped an elbow on the computer desk, "I might be able to help you if you told me what you were looking for."

Sarah sat up straight in her seat, a look of stubborn reticence flashed in her eyes as she looked down at her fidgeting fingers. She looked back up at Carl, but said nothing.

He weighed his words carefully before speaking, "Sarah, I'd be happy to help you find whatever...or whoever it is that you are looking for, but I need you trust me and share a little information with me."

"I don't even know you. Why should I tell you anything?"

Carl looked around the library and then back at Sarah, "I don't see anyone else here willing to help, and judging by the desperation written on your face, you could use a little help right now."

Sarah wanted to run away. She wanted to just leap from her chair, burst out the door, and drive back to New Hampshire. Her hours of research had turned up nothing. She should just give up before anyone found out about this insanity.

Stubbornness battled doubt and won. She wouldn't give up without trying all avenues. Carl was correct. There were no other options.

She slumped against the back of her chair, a look of defeat in her posture, "You're right. I do need help. And before I say anything else, I need to tell you, I lied to you yesterday when I told you I was a reporter."

Carl barely suppressed a laugh, "I really didn't think you were."

Sarah laughed at her foolishness, "Of course you didn't. Why would you? I mean..."

Carl waved off her explanations, "Really, it's fine. I'm not upset about it."

Sarah was grateful for his understanding and began her story of Abby Morris moving to Manchester. She explained that her ex was now in a relationship with Abby and that she had an unexplainable fear for Thom since the two had started dating. Carl took all this in without a word. He simply listened to Sarah's story until she had caught him up to speed on why she was now in Bangor. After she finished, she looked toward the floor, her eyes filled with tears, "Do...do you think I'm crazy for coming all the way up here on something as silly as an uneasy feeling about this girl?"

Carl shook his head, "People have done stranger things."

"I know, but do you think I'm crazy?"

He put his hand on her shoulder hoping it would bring her some comfort, "No, I don't think you are crazy."

Sarah wiped her eyes to look at Carl, "Why not? Because right now I feel as nutty as they come."

Carl patted her arm, "I don't think you're crazy, and for one very important reason. I knew Abby Morris."

CHAPTER SEVEN

An autumn wind twisted around Richard as he stood at the center of Mystery Hill. A frown appeared permanently engraved into his features. His eyes rose to the sky now and again. With an old broomcorn top attached to a large tree limb Richard brushed the surface of the ancient stones. The Equinox was not far away. Even though Percy had not returned, Richard would prepare the stone circle, just in case.

The Indian's heart weighed heavily within his chest at his companion's continued absence. Percy was more than just a crow. He was Richard's link to another realm of reality, what most people would call heaven. Without his feathered partner, Richard worried his presence at Mystery Hill was pointless.

The snake's appearance in the center of the circle signaled evil was afoot, and Richard surmised Percy's absence signified it was his job to take care of that evil alone. He had to make the right decision without any help from the other side.

Richard propped himself against his broom and scanned the trees once again and exhaled. He just prayed he made the right choice.

∞

A sliver of sunlight broke into Abby's room, the bright ray landing crossways on her cheek. Abby groaned faintly as she reached diagonally across the bed. Her eyelids sprang open, exposing the green irises underneath. Fear rattled in her chest as she tried to speak, "Thom?"

No reply.

Abby thrust the blankets off her naked body and flung on her nightgown, which lay over the back of a nearby chair. She called for Thom again and received only silence. Her voice quivered as each unanswered call of his name echoed through the empty house.

Abby shoved the window blinds to one side, and scanned the parking lot outside her apartment. The silence in her head began to roar as she realized Thom's car was nowhere to be seen. She ran to the bed and tossed the comforter, the sheets, and finally Thom's pillow to the floor, as she desperately searched for a note that he might have left to explain his absence. There was nothing on the bed, so she stomped to the front door, hoping he might have attached a note to the knob. Nothing.

Abby's rage multiplied as she looked in every room for some clue as to where Thom had gone. She passed by her dresser and caught sight of her reflection, her eyes loaded with the anger that burned throughout her body. Her knuckles turned white as she squeezed her fists into two tightknit balls. The crack of breaking glass reached her ears, immediately followed by an explosion of tiny shards which rained around her. It took the sight of her bloody hand for her brain to register she had punched her hand into the mirror over her dresser.

Vicious fury raged just behind her eyes and quickly coursed through her entire body, settling into the openings of the lacerated flesh that covered her knuckles. Abby's anger boiled over as she screamed, not from the pain in her hand, but from the indignity of Thom slipping away without so much as a word.

Abby made her way to the bathroom, blood dripping from her cupped palm. The red fluid streamed in-between her fingers, her eyes locked onto the gory sight as the tiny rivers splashed against the basin's white porcelain. She turned on the water and ran the warm liquid over her wounds. Blood quickly pooled in the sink as she wrung her hands tightly together.

Small pieces of glass peppered around the edges of the drain as the warm water rose to a near scalding temperature, "You devious little bastard! How *dare* you sneak out on me!"

∞

Sarah stood outside the Eastern Maine Community College Library and watched smoke drift through the air as Carl puffed on a cigarette. He took a long, steady drag and let the gray cloud orbit above his head.

Sarah pointed at his pocket, still reeling from his earlier revelation, "May I have one of those?"

Carl dug out a pack of cigarettes and a lighter, and handed them to Sarah. She took out one, lit it quickly, and returned them to Carl's awaiting hand.

"So you are telling me that you went to school with Abby?"

Carl nodded, "We would have graduated together in '04, but she changed schools after our junior year. There were a lot of rumors about why she left, but like everything in high school, you take what you hear with a grain of salt."

"What exactly did you hear?"

Carl thumped the butt of his cigarette and continued, "Well, let's see. I heard she was pregnant. I heard she got kicked out and had to transfer," he took another puff, "I heard that she couldn't stand her mother's constant bitching and moved in with her grandmother. Hell, I even heard that she killed someone. So, take your pick. Whatever the reason, I do know this; Abby Morris was a troubled girl."

"So you did actually witness that she was troubled?"

Carl nodded as he pushed his cigarette butt into a nearby ashtray, "She had a temper that wouldn't quit. Once at an assembly in the lunchroom, I saw her get in a knockdown drag-out with a chick in the senior class. Abby shoved the girl into a glass display case and cut her arm up pretty bad."

Sarah took a final draw from her cigarette and tossed it toward the ashtray, "Anything else you can think of about her?"

Carl motioned Sarah back toward the library entrance, "Come back inside. It would be easier if I looked it up on the database."

The two made their way back to the computer Sarah had been using earlier and Carl landed himself in the chair. Sarah pulled up a seat as he plugged away at the keyboard for several seconds. An article from a local newspaper filled the monitor. The date across the top of the paper read *Friday, July 11, 2003*.

Sarah leaned toward the screen and began to read.

Friends and family of Jennifer Kelly continue to search for the missing teen that vanished a week ago after a Fourth of July party in Hampden, Maine.

The 17-year-old was reported to have left the party around 1am, according to friends.

Loved ones, led by Jennifer's father, Chris Kelly, combed areas of Hampden and Bangor, on Saturday.

Local police found Jennifer's 2000 white Ford Focus hatchback abandoned near the Penobscot River.

Jennifer's family is exhausted and frustrated with the lack of clues in the disappearance of their daughter.

Friends of Jennifer told local police that the party she attended on the Fourth of July, prior to her disappearance was held at 1701 Elm St.

Jennifer was last seen wearing a black T-shirt and ripped blue jeans. She is 5' 06", 115 lbs., has reddish brown hair and blue eyes.

Anyone with information regarding her whereabouts is asked to call the Hampden Police Station.

Sarah looked to Carl, a puzzled look on her face, "What does this have to do with Abby?"

"I was at this party in 2003. So was Abby. I know that a lot of us thought she had something to do with Jennifer's disappearance."

"You mean they never found her?"

Carl shook his head, "Nope. The only thing the police ever found was her car, and there was nothing inside that showed any kind of foul play."

Sarah crossed her arms across her chest, "So what do you think?"

"Well...I know that Abby and Jennifer hated one another, but then again, Abby didn't get along with many girls. I always thought it was a little odd that Abby ended up changing schools the next year. I also know that I wasn't the only one that thought she might have had something to do with it."

"The police never questioned her about it?"

Carl shrugged, "I have no clue. Probably. They questioned everyone who was at the party. When I left, Jennifer's car was still there, so I really wasn't much help to their investigation."

Sarah leaned back in her chair as she tried to process everything that Carl had told her.

Carl watched her intently weigh her options before he asked, "What are you going to do?"

Sarah pushed her brunette locks behind one ear as she heaved a sigh, "I'm not sure. I guess I could go to the police station and see if they have any information on this missing girl."

Carl scratched at the dark scruff on his chin, "You could try, but I wouldn't guarantee them giving you much information."

"Why is that?"

Carl shrugged as he stood and walked back to the table where he had left his textbooks, "Why would they? They don't know you."

Sarah followed him to his chair and took a seat beside him, "You're probably

E G GLOVER

right, but I have to try." She glanced at the open books in front of Carl. Her hands shot over her mouth and a high-pitched shriek leaked between her clasped fingers. She looked around the library, embarrassed at her sudden outburst. A couple of the library's patrons looked up from their studies and whispered quietly to one another before returning to their work.

Carl startled at Sarah's shrill, his eyes mirroring her sudden anxiety, "What the hell? Are you okay?"

Sarah grabbed the book in front of Carl and jabbed a finger on a photo in the center of the page. Her brain flashed back to the nightmares that had haunted her for several weeks. She swallowed hard a few times as she tried to hold back the tears burning in her eyes, "Where...what is this place?!"

Carl's face flooded with concern as he took in the cloud of fear that manifested over Sarah's expression. He placed a hand on hers, "Why? Is it important?"

Sarah turned sharply toward him, her voice echoing within the library, "Dammit Carl, I'm serious. What is this place?"

Carl finally answered, "It's called Mystery Hill."

CHAPTER EIGHT

Thom sat with his back against a tall oak overlooking a small creek. He watched as a single leaf drifted through the air and delicately landed on the water's surface. Circular ripples radiated from the leaf's edges as it began its long journey downstream.

He knew there would be hell to pay when Abby realized he had slipped out this morning. A feeling inside Thom told him it was time to make some changes, and that ignited a fear he could no longer ignore.

Thom's sleep had been tormented with images of a large crow flying high above him, this time circling him like prey. He would try to hide behind rows of massive stones that littered the area around him, but this seemed to infuriate the bird even more.

Thom could see Abby standing in the distance, surrounded by a dense fog. She beckoned to him, her arms outstretched and her lips moving. But the sound of her voice was lost in the impenetrable air. Each time Thom moved toward Abby, the crow would swoop for his head. An attack cry erupted from its beak with Thom's every move. He positioned himself in a squatting stance, hoping to make himself less of a target.

Behind Thom, he could hear a voice calling to him, but the fog was too thick. It muted and distorted the voice just enough to make locating its owner impossible. It was a soft, soothing tone that kept repeating his name and pleaded with him to follow. He knew the familiar sound of Sarah's voice as it resonated across the wind.

As a last-ditch effort, he tried to attack his winged assailant with a branch he found lying on the leaf-covered stone floor. The branch weighed several times more than what it should have as he attempted to swat the creature from the air. Thom fell to the ground, and the dream came to an abrupt close just as the bird latched its razor sharp talons into his throat.

Thom once again focused on the solo leaf as it drifted down the stream, a name still lingering on his dry lips, "Sarah."

∞

Water mixed with blood splattered across the mirror in Abby's bathroom as she vigorously shook her wounds in an attempt to sling the pain from her injured hand. She threw open the cabinet door below the sink and grabbed a roll of gauze. Small pieces of mirror still bulged from her swollen knuckles as she uncoiled the white dressing around the still-bleeding openings in her flesh.

Small droplets of blood slowly dried on her cheeks as she ranted wildly, her eyes widened with the mania that continued to take control of her, "You tricky little shit! Slipping out while I'm asleep! Do you really think you can treat me like that without consequence?"

Abby stumbled out of the bathroom as her suppressed derangement worked its way through the mental barrier she maintained for so long. A thin crimson trail followed her into the living room, her balance compromised from the loss of blood. The couch caught her foot when she entered the room, which sent her to the floor in an unseemly heap.

Using her arms, she gradually pulled her body upright, and spied her cellphone sitting on the coffee table. Her surroundings spun around her, but she managed to grab the phone with an exasperated swipe. Taking a few steps forward, she lurched toward the front door and managed to grasp the doorknob. Searing pain traveled up her arm as she gave the handle a twist with her bandaged hand.

Her tirade continued as she slammed the door behind her, "You were sneaking over to some bitch's house, weren't you? Every chance you could! No wonder you lost your job! You overslept, but not because of nightmares! It was because you were skipping out on me to go screw around with some slut!"

Still wearing only her nightgown, Abby made her way to her car and fell into the driver's seat, "But don't you worry, Thom. I'll fix this for us. I will fix it. I'll take care of it all and we will be happy again! I love you, you'll see!"

Abby held the phone up to her face, her bandage turning from sterile white to a dark crimson. She carefully dialed Thom's number, placed the phone to her ear, and waited.

The call went straight to voicemail and she flung the phone toward the passenger seat with a growl, its backing and battery scattering across the car.

Abby's labored breathing cast a haze on the windshield as she sped toward Thom's apartment, her radio roaring at full volume.

∞

The words Mystery Hill reverberated in Sarah's ears in tempo with her pulse. She felt lightheaded, still staring at the open textbook with tears in her eyes. Her lungs grew tight, suffocating from anxiety, until the picture was slid out from under her view.

Carl quickly gathered up his books, placed them in his backpack, and escorted the thunderstruck Sarah outside the library to a decorative wrought iron bench. Her face had turned a near-colorless tint as he tried to retrieve a response from the girl, "Sarah? What is it? Are you okay?"

She turned her head toward him, her eyes glazed over as though she were looking through him.

Carl snapped his fingers near her ear, "Sarah? What the hell is wrong with you? What's so special about Mystery Hill?"

As if the words sparked a memory in her brain, she latched onto his outstretched hand and squeezed his fingers together, "Give me that book!"

Carl held the strap of his bag tightly, "Not until you tell me what is going on!"

Sarah rested her face in her hands and began to sob silently. She felt as if her sanity was being ripped away from her in large chunks. Wave after wave of emotion surged through her, until the sensation finally ceased and was replaced with a calming numbness.

She pushed away the tears from her cheeks and finally spoke, "I have seen that place in the photo many times."

The expression on Carl's face was expectant, "And...?"

Sarah pointed at his backpack, "That place in your book, I have been having dreams about it for weeks. I've never been there; I've never even heard the name Mystery Hill in my life! But yet, almost every time I fall asleep, I go to that place. And it's not just the stone circle. In the dreams there is this bird…a huge crow that flies around me. Like it's calling me to this place."

Carl unzipped his bag and removed the textbook. He flipped through its pages until he got to the photo that Sarah had seen earlier. Another page turn revealed a different picture of Mystery Hill.

He handed the book to her and pointed at the picture, "You mean this?"

When Sarah looked down at the book, she gasped at the sight. It was a black and white photo of a large, moss-covered stone. The sun could be seen setting in an opening in the trees, and there, resting on the rock's peak, was the animal that had followed her in her dreams for so many nights.

Sarah quickly read the pages that covered the subject of Mystery Hill.

Mystery Hill - America's Stonehenge

America's Stonehenge is an archaeological site consisting of a number of large rocks and stone structures scattered around roughly thirty acres within the town of Salem, New Hampshire. It is estimated to be somewhere on the border of four thousand years old.

At its center is a large circle of stones with two ten foot tall, vertical stones on the east and west edges that mark the spring and autumn equinoxes.

A number of hypotheses exist as to the origin and purpose of the structure. One legend suggests that it is a kind of portal, allowing persons to travel to different places in time. However, little is known on how someone could use the circle in order to make such a journey.

It has been said that some people who visited the site experienced moments of 'missing time'.

For example, a lady from New York claimed she went up on the hill to explore the stone structure, an endeavor that should have taken a couple of hours. Upon returning to her car, however, she discovered that almost six hours had passed.

Of course, there is no proof that this event actually occurred. Most stories of the *odd events at the site have been written off as legend or hearsay.*

Sarah slammed the book closed and handed it back to Carl, "So, it is a real place after all. I need you to make me a copy of those pages. Could you do that for me?"

Carl looked down at the book and bounced its weight in his hand as he tried to make sense of Sarah's story, "Yeah, I can get a photocopy in the library, but I really don't understand. Does this have anything to do with Abby?"

Sarah smiled when she realized how crazy all of this must sound to Carl. She tried to cover up her frantic fear, "I'm sorry, Carl. No, this doesn't have anything to do with Abby. It's just me being silly. I get a little carried away sometimes."

Carl looked at her with skepticism in his gaze, "But what about your dreams? You were certain you had seen that stone circle in..."

Sarah cut him short, "It's nothing. Really, I'm okay."

"Are you sure?"

Sarah nodded. She could tell Carl didn't believe her, but it really didn't matter. She had other things to attend to other than trying to convince him of her wellbeing.

Carl sighed as he stood and motioned the textbook toward her, "You still want me to copy this?"

Sarah replied with a half-smile, "Please."

"Okay. I'll be right back."

Carl turned and disappeared into the library. Sarah rested her chin in her hands while she weighed her options. This trip had turned into more than just a way to smear dirt on Abby's reputation. The creeping evil that had inundated her sleep for weeks just cemented into a terrifying reality.

Sarah watched as Carl returned with a handful of papers stapled, his backpack tossed over one shoulder. He offered the stack to her, "I took the liberty of circling the section that shows Mystery Hill's location in New Hampshire."

Sarah took the papers and Carl retrieved a cigarette from his pack, "So, what are going to do next? Go to the police and inquire about Jennifer Kelly?"

"Yes. Maybe I can find something out, I don't know."

Carl lit his cigarette, slid his lighter into his pocket, and offered her a hand, "Well, good luck Sarah. I hope you find whatever it is that you are looking for."

Sarah took his hand as she rose from the bench, her eyes full of gratitude, "Thank you for all your help. I wouldn't have found anything without you." She leaned toward him, gave him a small kiss on the cheek and a hug, and quickly retreated to her car before he could say another word.

The sensations that burned in Sarah's heart were too much for her to handle. She needed to be alone. Carl had been a godsend, but she couldn't hide her emotional state from him any longer. Seeing the picture of Mystery Hill had all but sent her over the edge.

CHAPTER NINE

The GPS on Sarah's phone had led her straight to the Hampden police station. Her hands were still shaking from her discovery, but she had to put that behind her long enough to speak to someone about the disappearance of Abby's classmate eleven years ago. It was difficult to bury the images of Mystery Hill she had seen in Carl's textbook, but as she parked her car in front of the police station, she knew it was time to let them go...at least temporarily.

Sarah straightened her hair and touched up her makeup in her car's rearview before she approached the door.

She made her way up a set of stone steps, paused at the door, and took in a deep breath as she pulled on the handle to reveal a police officer seated on a stool behind a chest-high counter. The officer's eyes were pointed downward as he flipped through a collection of papers.

Sarah stepped to the counter and waited for him to take notice of her presence. After several seconds, the man spoke, his eyes still glued to his paperwork, "Can I help you?"

Sarah began the speech she had rehearsed once before, "Hello. My name is Sarah Wisdom and I was wondering if it were possible for me to get some information on a missing person's case from eleven years ago?"

The man stopped what he had been doing looked up at Sarah with an irritated expression on his face, "You want to do what?"

Sarah could feel her nervousness about to bubble over as she tried to repeat her question, "I'm looking into a missing person's case from eleven years ago, a girl by the name of Jennifer Kelly. I was wondering if I could get any information about..."

He quickly looked back to his paperwork and let out an annoyed sigh, "Are you a family member of this missing person?"

Sarah stammered slightly, "Well no, but…"

"We aren't allowed to give out any information unless you are a direct relation to the person in question."

Sarah tried to insist, "But I figured since the case was several years old I could talk to someone about the events of…"

The officer lifted his head sharply, "Look lady…what was your name? Ms. Wisdom? We don't have time to dig around in a cold case from over a decade ago! If you want information on the disappearance of this girl, I recommend you contact her next of kin. Otherwise, I guess you're outta luck!"

The officer looked down once again and acted as though Sarah wasn't in the room.

Sarah stormed out of the police station and made her way back to her car.

∞

Another policeman walked up behind the officer who sat on the stool and tapped him on the shoulder, "Hey Roberts, what the hell was that all about?"

The older man scoffed, "Some kid wanting to dig around in a missing person's case from 2003. I told her to contact the girl's next of kin."

The younger officer rubbed his thumb and forefinger across his ginger mustache, "Really? Which missing person's case?"

Roberts looked back at him and rolled his eyes, "Hell Morris, what does it matter? We got enough to keep up with as it is! I think she said Kelly, Jennifer Kelly. We couldn't have helped her anyway. The girl wasn't a direct relative, said her last name was Wisdom. Now get back to work!"

The young officer made a mocking salute and went back to his desk.

Morris picked up a pencil and tapped it anxiously on the stack of papers in front of him as he stared at the phone on his desk, "My God, Abby. It's finally happened."

∞

Abby stood on her tiptoes, her arm outstretched as her fingers probed cautiously along the frame of Thom's front door. She had witnessed Thom hide the thin, black box a month ago, she'd just never had to use it. The edge of her forefinger found her prize and she pushed it upward until the rectangular object fell to the ground. She gleefully grasped the container and slid open one side to reveal a spare key to Thom's apartment.

The key entered the lock smoothly as Abby gave the knob a quick twist and hurried inside the opening. She pushed the door closed and collapsed on the nearby couch.

She cuddled one of the couch's throw pillows and pulled her legs close to her body. She sighed with contentment as she buried her face deeper into the overstuffed pillow, surrounded by the comforting smell of Thom's cologne.

Abby rolled to one side and caught sight of her bare legs. She gasped in horror to realize she was still in her nightgown and quickly jumped to her feet. She marched into Thom's bedroom and pulled open the top drawer of his dresser. She tossed various articles of his clothing behind her as she looked for something to wear. She knew she had left a few of her clothes here and rummaged through every drawer until she found a top and a pair of jeans. Thom's clothes lay strewed around his bedroom as Abby plucked off her nightgown and slid into her new-found clothing.

Abby looked at the bandage on her hand, trying hard to remember exactly how it had gotten there. She strolled to the bathroom, located a fresh roll of gauze, and proceeded to unroll the blood-dried dressing that encased her hand.

She winced in agony with each twist of her wrist as she slowly revealed the gory sight that used to be her knuckles. Slivers of glass gleamed in her skin and the freshly open wounds began to bleed once more. The cloth dropped to the floor in a bloody, crinkled lump.

Abby dug into a drawer under the sink and fished out a pair of tweezers. Each yank of the small instrument caused a shockwave of pain up her arm, but eradicated the small fragments of shattered mirror deep from her knuckles. Fresh crimson cascaded down the length of her fingers and dripped into the sink's basin below.

Once all the glass was removed, Abby found a container of alcohol. She unscrewed the lid and held her breath as she washed the clear liquid over her awaiting hand. The burn that followed caused Abby to produce a near primeval shriek, triggering her to flex her lacerated knuckles into a tight fist.

Tears pooled in Abby's eyes and she blinked rapidly as the pain subsided. She found a tube of triple antibiotic ointment and smeared it generously on her wounds. The cool cream somewhat smothered the alcohol burn and Abby's muscles gradually began to relax. She took the fresh gauze, wrapped her hand neatly, and attached the gauze with a metal clip. Abby smiled down at her work.

"There! Much better," was all she uttered.

She patted at the pockets of her jeans and realized she didn't have her phone and hoped it was in her car.

Barefooted, Abby exited the apartment and opened her car door to find her phone in three separate pieces. The phone's facing, back cover, and battery were in various areas of the floorboard. She scratched at her head, trying to remember how her cell had ended up in such a state; but she couldn't recall. She also found her car keys in the ignition and plucked them from their resting place.

Abby pieced her phone back together and returned to Thom's apartment. She had no memory of the morning, and that plagued her.

She slid the back of her cellphone over its battery and held down the power button until the screen lit up. She perched herself on Thom's couch and retrieved the television remote from the end table. As she flipped through the channels, her phone chirped to alert her there was an awaiting voicemail.

Abby sat down the remote and squealed out loud, "Oh, I bet it's Thom!" The caller's name scrolled across the cellphone's screen in bold letters: *Kyle Morris*.

Abby's expression went blank and she placed the phone to her awaiting ear.

∞

Sarah pressed the button on her cruise control as she headed south on Interstate 95. Her futile attempt at the police station had her fuming with anger; not just at the arrogant indifference of the police officer, but also at herself. She tried to believe her trip to Maine hadn't been a gigantic waste of her time, but she knew better. At best, all she could tell Thom about was Abby's shady reputation. For all the good it would do. She knew it would come across as just a jealous ex-girlfriend's effort to cause havoc in his new relationship; and she knew even that part was fairly accurate.

This trip had been Sarah's last effort to somehow persuade Thom back to her side of the fence. Her returning with nothing more than a handful of decade old rumors wasn't going to sway Thom's affections. But that was not all she had uncovered.

The information Sarah accidently found from Carl about Mystery Hill had her positively petrified...but enthralled, all at the same time. Had it really been an accident she had found Carl's textbook covering the whereabouts of her reoccurring nightmares...or were they visions?

Sarah drummed on her steering wheel as she watched the approaching overpass cast dark shadows over her car. She knew she still had Jesse covering for her at work and that made her choice only that much more simple. Her foot pressed the accelerator a bit harder as she reset her cruise control. She was going to Mystery Hill.

∞

Richard stepped outside and scanned the horizon; the sky above him was grey with contempt. He looked all around his office building, and even walked around to the back, passed the seldom used spare bedroom window where Percy sometimes liked to perch himself on dreary days. His friend was still missing.

He scratched at his chin, wondering, as he propped against the side of the building. He looked up the side of the hill, occasionally shifting his head in hopes of catching a black streak cutting through the air to land on his shoulder.

The Indian had all but given up hope of ever seeing the crow again, and the Equinox was tomorrow evening. He had readied the stone circle, like he had always done, hoping it would bring back Percy. But it was to no avail.

Richard was still perplexed as to why he had been blessed with his newly acquired youth. Had it been a tradeoff for the loss of his companion?

Tears started to fill Richard's eyes as he took a deep breath. He looked high in the air once more, "Tabaldak was correct with His warning of the future. Perhaps I should have listened more closely."

CHAPTER TEN

The phone shook in Abby's hand as she fixated on the message waiting in her voicemail box. Her bottom lip quivered at the sound of her brother's tone.

"Abby, it's Kyle. We need to talk! Call me back as soon as you get this! Don't wait, don't think about it, just do it!" The message ended with a hollow click from his side of the recording.

Abby's face had gone grey as she lowered the phone and looked at its keypad. Kyle rarely called her, and when he did, it was usually to bitch her out about some deed she'd done that he deemed reckless and impulsive. She knew by the urgency in his voice, this call wasn't the usual theatrics.

Abby traced her fingernail along the edges of the phone's number pad, debating the call. The phone buzzed and chirped deafeningly, and she tossed it away in horror, surprised at its ringing.

Abby caught her breath and retrieved the phone from the floor, eyeing the Caller ID. She reluctantly pressed the answer button, "Yeah," being her simple greeting.

Kyle's voice thundered from the small speaker, "Why the hell didn't you call me back?"

Abby groaned in response, "I just got your message. What do you want?"

"You got problems."

Abby chuckled half-heartedly into her cell, "Ha! Tell me something I don't already know."

Kyle was silent for a moment, "No! I mean you've got big problems, and they are probably headed your way right now!"

She scoffed at her brother's usual dramatic performance.

He continued, "Some girl was up here, asking about Jennifer Kelly's disappearance."

Abby held her breath at the name, "Okay. So what?"

"I didn't talk to her, one of the other officer's did. Said her last name was Wisdom. You know anyone by that name?"

The phone slipped from Abby's hand and bounced to the floor. Her brother's voice could still be heard rumbling from it, but none of the words reached Abby's ears.

Abby stood up and with the rage of a rabid bull began throwing and breaking every object within her reach. Lamps, picture frames, wall clocks, small furniture, any object she could pick up, none stood a chance.

The sound of her brother's voice finally reached her ears as he shouted at her from the fallen cellphone. Abby zeroed in on his yelling, and pounced on the phone with all her might, her heels breaking the phone into small plastic chunks.

Abby stormed out of the apartment and jumped into her car, "So that little mousy-haired whore has been trying to dig out dirt on me? She has no clue who the hell she's messing with!"

The car roared to life and Abby shoved it into gear. The tires spun wildly until finally gaining traction on the pavement. Abby continued to talk to the air, "I know where you live, Sarah. You'll be sorry you ever knew my name!"

∞

I wanted to fly, on the winds in high climb,
Until my mind was free.
But then I hit a wall, and began to fall,
My eyes were too blind to see.

Sarah sat chewing on a cheeseburger while the music from the radio filled the interior of her car. She took a sip from her drink and sighed with contentment. She had not eaten since yesterday, her stomach deciding for her that it was time for a pit stop.

Between bites, Sarah checked her GPS and learned she was within twenty minutes of Mystery Hill. While she ate, she watched the sun sink on the horizon and the lights in the fast food parking lot switch on. Their beams illuminated the area around her as she took the last bite of her burger.

Sarah wadded her empty sandwich wrapper into a ball and tossed it into the empty bag in her passenger seat. She took another sip from her straw while cautiously backing out of the parking space, directing her car back toward the interstate.

The music continued on the car's radio, her anxiety triggering an undeniable tightness in her chest.

Hands of time,
Keep reaching out for me.
Reaching, but never touching me.

Sarah knew it was time to confront her nightmares.

∞

A feeling of dread washed over Thom as he pulled into the parking lot of his apartment complex. Two police cars sat outside, their red and blue strobe lights reflecting off the building's windows. He could see that his apartment door was open and he quickly exited his car.

Thom approached the entrance just as a uniformed officer stepped outside, "What's going on?" Thom's voice vibrated with alarm.

The broad policeman took a step back and blocked the opening, "Is this your apartment?"

Thom tried to see around the officer's bulk, but the man clearly had no intention of letting him look inside, "Yes, it is. What's happened?"

"That's what we'd like to know. We got a call from one of your neighbor's that it sounded like someone was tearing the place apart."

"I've not been home since late yesterday."

The policeman jabbed his open palm at Thom, "Can I see your identification, please?"

Thom was dumbfounded, but complied, dug his wallet from his back pocket, and dropped his ID into the man's awaiting hand.

The officer studied it carefully, handed it back to him, and took a step back, "Okay, come in, but watch your step. There's a lot of broken glass in the floor," he then yelled toward the bed, "Hey Campbell, the guy that lives here just showed up!"

Another policeman walked from the bedroom, quickly looked Thom over and nodded, then disappeared back into the room.

Thom scanned his living room for the first time and groaned with anguish, "Oh my God! What...who did this?"

"We were hoping you might be able to tell us. You know anyone that'd want to wreck all your stuff?"

Thom's eyes grew to the size of saucers as he looked at all the damage. Everything was either upside down or broken into pieces.

"Mr. Collier?"

Thom's attention snapped back to the question in the air, "Um...no, not really, no."

He quickly filed through his thoughts, trying to decide who would be the most likely candidate for the madness that lay scattered all around him. The first thought that came to mind was Sarah, but this carnage was way over the top. It was incomprehensible.

Thom paced around the broken remains of his living room and stepped back to his bedroom. He nodded to the other officer.

"Whoever did this decided to take a look through your dresser. Your clothes have been thrown all over the room. We also found a bloody bandage in the bathroom floor. You know anything about that?"

Thom shook his head, still trying to process the destruction that was once his apartment, "Like I told the other officer, I haven't been home." He scratched at the back of his head as his shock took ahold of his senses.

Glass crunched under his feet as he returned to the living room. He flipped his recliner back to its upright position and fell into it.

The first policeman stood nearby as he wrote into a small notebook, "I know it may be hard to tell, but does it look like anything is missing?"

He did another scan of the room's wreckage, "No, it doesn't look like anything is missing. Just trashed." It was then that he noticed something on the floor, something that was not his.

Thom pushed himself from his chair and walked over to inspect the broken object near his couch. With a tap of his shoe he flipped the small article over and recognized it immediately, Abby's cellphone.

CHAPTER ELEVEN

Richard bolted from under his old quilt and ran to the bedroom window. The sound of an approaching car had roused him from his half-asleep state. He pushed up the lower sash in time to see a set of headlights as they bobbed up and down the driveway and stopped in front of the office porch. The thick smell of summer's end flooded his senses before he slid the window closed.

He caught a quick glance of the clock that rested on his nightstand as he reached for a pair of faded jeans that were draped over the back of a chair. It was just a few minutes past eleven. He wondered who would be calling so late in the evening.

Richard cautiously peered from his window and scrutinized the shape that approached the office door. The fog was considerable, and it took him a moment to realize it was a young, brunette girl that had arrived on his front stoop. He judged from her demeanor she was fairly apprehensive about her surroundings.

He eased the door open before she had a chance to knock, and greeted her with a friendly smile, "Hello miss. Is everything okay?"

The young girl jumped slightly and looked as though she were about to bolt back into her car, so Richard tried to offer a few more kind words, "If you are lost, I might be able to help."

After a few seconds, she succeeded in choking out a response, "No...I'm not lost," she laughed nervously, "Actually, I feel like I've been here many times before."

Richard's smile only widened, "Well miss, perhaps you have. Mystery Hill is a very magical place. Would you like to come into my office and have a seat? You could tell me about it."

She hesitated, "I don't know if..."

Richard tried to wave off her barely caged restraint, "It's okay. You aren't the first to be drawn here," he opened the door wide and let her look inside, "We have visitors often."

The young lady looked inside the office as Richard stepped back from the opening. After nearly a minute, she stepped over the threshold and examined the room further. Richard slid himself behind his desk and reached for his favorite pipe. He glanced over at Percy's usual perching spot and felt grief return to his heart.

"Please, have a seat. My name is Richard Adahy. What's your name?"

She took one last gaze around the office and sat in the seat across from him, "Sarah Wisdom."

Richard stood slightly and offered his hand, which she took and gave a small shake, "Pleased to meet you, Sarah."

Sarah nodded halfheartedly and released his hand.

"So, what brings you to Mystery Hill on such a gloomy night?"

Sarah's face grew solemn as Richard waited for her to speak. Her words came hesitantly, "My...nightmares."

The Indian lit his pipe and released a thick cloud that rose above his head, "You've had dreams about this place then?"

Sarah, surrounded by a thick layer of apprehension, nodded her response.

Richard grinned at her in hopes he could calm her nervousness, "There's no reason to be afraid of the dreams you've been having. It means you are one of a very small group of people that have been chosen to travel within the circle."

"What exactly do you mean by 'travel'?"

"Mystery Hill is a doorway, a path to the past and to the future. You have the ability to travel through this doorway."

Sarah scoffed at the Indian's words, "Surely you can't be serious?"

Richard shrugged, "What do you think? Do you think it is mere coincidence that you have had dreams of this place, over and over again, by your account, and now you find yourself here?"

Sarah thought hard and finally answered, "No, I don't."

"If a person who truly believes stands in the center of the stone circle on the evening of the fall equinox, they will actually step into the days long past."

Sarah's fear slowly flowed out of her body, chased away by a spark of nervous hope brought on by Richard's words.

"But, I do need you to understand, there is a risk. If it is done incorrectly, you could be trapped in an endless second of time, with no past and no future," Richard took another draw from his pipe, "but that is why I am here, to help you on your way."

Richard continued to enjoy his pipe while Sarah sat motionless for several minutes. The emotions that flew across her open face told him she was weighing her options carefully. As he studied the young girl, he struggled to blow away his worry with each puff out from his pipe. The Indian had never attempted to send someone into the void without Percy in attendance. His lack of confidence in himself was wearing on his soul, but he refused to let the fear within him take control. He knew he had the strength to do what he was destined to do.

Sarah looked at Richard with determination in her eyes, "I'll do it. I'll go. What do I need to do?"

Richard's eyes mirrored hers, "First, I need to know where you are you wanting to go, future or past?"

Sarah's reply came before Richard's words had completely left his lips, "The past. I'm going to fix what happened with my ex that was caused by an outside source. I know with all my heart that he and I are supposed to be together. It wasn't until this girl from out of state arrived and screwed everything up that our destiny together was derailed. If I can go back and change that, I'm confident our lives will take the course originally meant."

Richard questioned her once more, "Are you sure?"

Sarah answered without a moment's hesitation, "I'm positive!"

Richard sat down his pipe and walked to the door as he motioned her to follow, "Then come with me."

Her eyes widened, "Where? Outside? It's the middle of the night!"

He reached over to a table and pulled open a small drawer to reveal a long, black flashlight, "I got it covered," and smiled with a wink.

Sarah returned the grin with an eager one of her own and followed Richard outside as he clicked the button on the large torch. She followed closely behind him as he led the way up the path until they reached the hill's zenith.

The fog was much thicker at the top of Mystery Hill, which made Sarah huddle that much closer to Richard's back. Richard could feel the apprehension radiate off her body with each step into the dense fog. He paused and turned to face her, the young girl's face illuminated in the beam of his flashlight, "We don't have to continue. We could wait until daylight."

Sarah vigorously shook her head, "No, I want to go. I have to see this place in person."

Richard gave her a quick nod and continued toward the large circle of stones, the fog still thickening around them. His heart ached for the grip of Percy's talons on his shoulder. Mystery Hill had become a different place without the presence of his guide.

Through the fog, they approached one of the large stones and Richard felt Sarah's emotions intensify, and then gradually relax. He stopped again and shined his light toward the ground, "Watch your step. The ground becomes stone at this point. Don't let it trip you up in the fog."

Sarah didn't speak; she just followed Richard's lead. He watched her reaction in the dim light as the stones encased their path on their way to the circle's center. There was no sound, no wind. Everything was completely still in the near-impenetrable fog.

The two of them reached the center and Richard shined his light in all directions, "Here is the place that has filled your dreams. Your visions of Mystery Hill have been a summoning, showing you where you were destined to come."

Sarah didn't acknowledge his words, though he was certain she heard them. She just stood, transfixed at her surroundings. A tear slid down her cheek and she let out a stifled laugh.

After several minutes of staring into the night, she turned to Richard, "What do I need to do?"

Richard placed a hand on her shoulder and beamed at the strength of her determination, "I want you to go home and rest easy tonight. I will need you to come back here thirty minutes before sunset. It is extremely important you arrive on time. Do you understand?"

Sarah nodded her understanding, "I will be here on time."

Richard observed Sarah with a shared emotional understanding as they made their way back down the path of Mystery Hill. He pointed the light at the door of her car and watched as she slid behind the wheel, "Be safe and I will see you tomorrow."

Sarah drove away while Richard watched the fog swallow her vehicle, until even its taillights vanished into the night. He took a step toward the office porch, and viewed Percy's usual perching spot on the roof's edge. All that rested there was darkness.

∞

The headlights of Sarah's car cast an eerie shadow against the fog when she turned off the road that led to Richard's office. Her emotions leapt between relieved and terrified as she tried to make sense of the conversation she'd just had with the pipe-smoking stranger.

If it had not been for her dreams and the Indian's anomalous ability to calm a large portion of her fears, she would never return to Mystery Hill. The vibes of peace and understanding he cast around her were almost inebriating.

Sarah hoped she would finally get a night's rest without being barraged with fragmented images of real life events, mixed with visions of the mysterious stone circle. Richard had told her to rest, and that was exactly what she intended to do.

She continued toward the highway as the fog around her gradually began to lift, hand in hand with her anxiety. It was a forty-five minutes' drive to Sarah's apartment, and her bed was calling her name.

CHAPTER TWELVE

The jagged edges of the broken glass poked at Abby's forearm as she reached through the window. The click from the latch snapping open resounded in the dark room on the other side of the sash. She carefully slid the window upward and crawled over the sill. As quietly as she could manage, she closed the window and relocked the metal catch.

Abby waited for her eyes to adjust to the darkness that enveloped her, and chuckled with accomplishment at gaining entry to Sarah's apartment. Once she was accustomed to the dark, she located the large rock she had used to break the window. Abby snatched the rock from the floor, lobbed it in the air once, and caught it with her bandaged hand and smirked, "Worked like a charm."

With one spin around the room, she plopped herself on Sarah's couch. Her eyes still gleamed from her ingenuity at getting into the apartment, "Sarah's going to be so surprised when she gets home." She giggled at the thought of parking her car in an adjacent parking lot; no one would notice she was at Sarah's apartment

Abby's shine quickly faded when she recalled the conversation with her brother. She couldn't believe that Sarah had traveled to Bangor to find out things about her past. How Sarah had managed to find out about Jennifer Kelly's disappearance had Abby dumbfounded, "How could she possibly know? That was such a long ago. How could she know I had something to do with it?"

Abby rolled the rock back and forth in her hands, the memories of that summer in 2003 slowly leaked back into her memory...

∞

Friday, July 4, 2003...

Abby approached Matt's door. Her green dress fitted snugly, complementing her youthful curves. She was radiating with excitement at being invited to this party, and had bought the dress especially for it. She just hoped Matt would notice.

Her finger pressed lightly on the doorbell and a tall, muscular fellow opened the door. His black hair was pushed to one side, barely covering one eye. But even with his bangs partially obstructing his view, Abby could tell he liked what he saw.

"Abby! You made it! Damn girl, you are looking fine tonight," Matt admired as he motioned her inside.

She grinned at him with a slight look of seduction in her gaze, "Thanks," was all she said, and gave him a wink.

Abby had been crushing on Matt ever since their freshmen year, so him asking her to come and hang out at his house while his parents were out of town, had her confidence at an all-time high.

"Can I get you something to drink," he quizzed as she walked into the living room with a half a dozen other people from their junior class.

She thought for a minute as she started to sit down, "Do you have anything sweet?"

"Yeah, several sweet drinks. Come in the kitchen and I will let you pick," Matt answered, walking into the living room and taking her by the hand.

Abby could tell by the smell of him, Matt had already had a few drinks, most likely beer. She allowed him to lead her into the kitchen, and he opened a cabinet next to the refrigerator. She whistled at what she saw, "Wow! That's a lot of liquor!"

Abby was an old pro at alcohol, but she figured it would look good to Matt if he thought she was a little dense on the subject, "I don't really know what to pick. What would you recommend?"

Matt slid up next to her in front of the cabinet, placing his hand on her side, "Amaretto is a good one, it's sweet."

Abby smiled at him and agreed, "Okay, I'll try that one, but not too much."

"Oh no, of course not," his slurred voice making it obvious how much he had drank before her arrival.

Abby looked out the back door while Matt made her drink, and saw a familiar face looking back at her through the glass. It was Jennifer, a girl she had known all throughout high school, and hated with a passion.

"What is she doing here," ran through Abby's head just as the back door sprang open.

The look on Jennifer's face was one of contempt, her blue eyes filled with fury, "Abby? Can I speak to you for a minute?"

Matt turned toward the auburn haired girl, his cheerful look fading away as he spilt some of the liquor on his hand.

Abby's heart lit up with a familiar cockiness as she took the full glass from Matt's hand, downed its contents, and stepped outside with Jennifer.

The two girls treaded away from the back porch and to one side of the house, near Abby's car. Abby was already feeling the effects of the liquor, which just served to light the flame of wrath that stayed constantly kindled within her.

Before Abby could speak, Jennifer started screeching at her, "I don't know what you think you are doing here, but Matt is *my* boyfriend!"

Abby huffed in reply, "From what I've heard, you think *everyone's* your boyfriend! Matt dumped your ass six months ago."

Jennifer ignored Abby's comment and continued, "You think you can march your skanky ass in here and try to take my man, bitch? I've got some news for you!"

Abby quickly glanced around her and took notice of a baseball bat propped against the bricks of the house wall. Without a moment's hesitation, she picked up the bat and swung it with all her might into the side of Jennifer's head. She didn't have time to make a sound as the wood made contact with her temple. Abby stood over Jennifer and added another blow to the side of her head before she was satisfied.

Abby then walked smirking and confident to her car, opened the trunk, and tossed the bat inside. She then grabbed Jennifer by the length of her long hair and dragged her the few feet required to get her body to the edge of her trunk.

Abby lifted the girl's small frame with no difficulty and shoved her headfirst into the opening, and closed the lid with a slight press of her palm.

Without so much as a thought, she returned to the back porch and into the kitchen. She found Matt looking through the liquor cabinet for another bottle. He paused when he heard the back door open and turned to look at Abby, "Where'd Jenn go?"

Abby flashed her special smile and winked at him once again, "She said she was going home."

Matt's gaze was confused in his half-lit stupor, "Home?"

"Yeah. She said she wasn't going to deal with seeing me flirt with you all night."

Matt gave Abby a devilish smile and approached her, leaning in to steal a kiss.

"Nah-uh. Let me run to the restroom first," Abby winked and asked him to direct her to it.

Matt pointed the way and Abby walked down the hall, elated that Matt was showing her so much attention.

She stepped inside and closed the door, turning on the faucet to wash her hands. As she lathered the soap between her fingers, she stared into the mirror and checked her makeup; she wanted to look perfect for Matt if he was going to kiss her.

She straightened her hair just a touch as she made kissy faces at her reflection, "Too hot for *his* own good."

∞

Still in Sarah's apartment, Abby's body twitched as the old events came back to haunt her thoughts. She pulled her legs close to her body at the memory of her agitated call to her brother to help dispose of Jennifer's corpse.

After Abby had fished Jennifer's keys from her pocket, Kyle had driven Jennifer's car to Penobscot River. Abby had followed Kyle in her own car with the body of the young girl still in the trunk. Once the car was abandoned, Abby and Kyle traveled to a large hog farm a few hours away.

Abby watched as Kyle opened the trunk and unceremoniously pulled Jennifer's lifeless body from the dark recess. He dropped her to the dirt road and jerked her clothes from her small frame. Abby shuddered at the sight of Jennifer's naked form as Kyle tossed her clothes inside the car.

Abby threw her hands over her face as she relived the horror replaying in her mind. She remembered him saying he would burn the clothes and the bat so no one would find them. Kyle was a policeman. She knew he would know what to do.

After Kyle had removed all of her clothing, he told Abby to grab Jennifer's feet and they heaved the girl to the eagerly awaiting pigs. They squealed with delight at the unexpected free meal.

Tears streamed from Abby's eyes as she collapsed on the couch, the rock she had been holding slid from the couch and fell to the floor with a solid thud.

A sudden flash of headlights came in front of the window and went dark. Abby's eyes went wide as she heard the sound of a car door open and shut. She jumped to her feet, eyes manic with the insanity she had concealed in her mind for over a decade. She looked toward the front door and could see that the knob had started to rattle. It had to be Sarah coming home.

In one swift move, Abby grabbed the rock from the floor and positioned herself beside the door. As the opening swung inward, she lifted the rock above her head, and waited. It was still dark as she watched someone walk into the room and reach for the light switch. Abby held her breath as she aimed the rock and smashed it into the darkened figure's head.

CHAPTER THIRTEEN

Thom stood at his apartment door and watched as the two police cars exited the parking lot. He toyed with the card one of the officers had given him that had the police department's information printed across one side; the phone number was in bold print for him to call, just in case he needed to speak to anyone about the incident. He stepped back inside, acquired a large garbage bag from the kitchen, and began sifting through the remains of his living room.

Thom had kept his mouth shut about Abby's phone laying in pieces on the floor. He was fairly confident that the state of his apartment went hand in hand with him leaving her place without a word this morning. He knew Abby was full of passion, and that it leaked out in various forms, but if she had done the damage, he would deal with it himself rather than getting the police involved. After all, he did care about her, and revenge wasn't his style.

As Thom picked up the broken items scattered around his living room, he recalled his strange dreams about Abby and Sarah wandering around in the foggy midst of that forbidding stone circle. Had the dream been more than just a dream, perhaps a vision of the dilemma his heart had dealt with over the passing weeks? Either way, he was perplexed by the impact his dreams had on his emotions. His head ached as he tried to make sense of it all.

The garbage bag was nearly full as Thom fell into a sitting position on the couch. He surveyed the room and the few items that had not been destroyed. He pulled the draw string on the bag closed and headed toward his bedroom. Nothing seemed to be broken as he picked up his clothes that had been tossed about the room. He folded them up and placed them on his bed. The drawers of his dresser still hung open and he looked inside each one before pushing them back into place.

Thom examined the bottom drawer carefully; it was where he kept some antique jewelry that had belonged to his grandfather. It was also the home of the 9mm pistol he owned. None of the items were missing, which told him whatever happened in his apartment, it had definitely not been a mere robbery. Those items would have been easy pickings for any thief looking for a quick buck.

Thom removed the pistol from its resting place and sat it on the bed, before pushing the drawer closed. He'd not fired it in years, not since his grandfather had passed away, the man that had taught him how to use it. He stared at the weapon as it sat ominously on his bed. Thom had hoped he'd never have to use it, but after tonight, he was happy to have it with him, just in case Abby hadn't caused the damage, but been a victim.

Thom stepped to his hallway closet, found a small zippered bag, and returned to the bedroom. He examined the pistol for a moment, placed it inside the black container, and quickly zipped it closed. He started to return the gun to his bottom drawer, but thought otherwise. His gut told him to keep it close.

As Thom passed through the living room, he snatched up the loaded garbage bag near the couch and exited his apartment. He swung by the dumpster and tossed the trash inside before getting into his car. He placed the zippered tote with his pistol on the seat next to him and turned the key in the ignition. If Abby had really trashed his apartment, he thought it wise to go check in on her. Thom just hoped in Abby's unstable state she had not paid Sarah a visit.

∞

The room slowly came into focus, followed by a throb of agonizing pain as Sarah opened her eyes. The light from the ceiling fan burned her eyes until the pain sharply settled into the back of her head. She tried to lift one arm to examine the large knot she could feel growing behind her left ear, but something prevented her movement.

A voice rattled from behind her and sent a wave of fear up her spine, "Don't even think about moving, bitch! I've got you exactly where I want you!"

Sarah strained to find the source of the words that had reverberated in the room, but her arms and legs had been tightly wrapped with a thick cord and tied to one of her own kitchen chairs. She frantically tried to kick her legs free, but the bindings were so tight, she couldn't manage even the slightest motion away from the wooden chair.

A face filled with madness spun into view the moment Sarah's chair was twisted toward her tormentor. Abby stood with her head lowered to Sarah's level, her red hair frizzy and matted with perspiration. Abby's pupils were dilated so large Sarah could barely see any green in the irises.

Abby's tone was maniacal, though her face eerily expressionless, as she lilted to Sarah, "I hear you have been on a little trip to my home town! Did you enjoy your stay? You...you should have told me you were going, I could have shown you around!"

Sarah's plea leaked from her lips, "Abby, please...please stop this!"

Abby's vacant expression turned angry and her palm stung Sarah's cheek with a sharp strike. She screamed at the top of her lungs until her voice cracked under the stress, "Don't even speak to me! You don't know me!"

Sarah's lip quivered while tears rolled down her face as she tried not to make another sound which might send Abby to the next level of psychosis.

"I moved to Manchester to get away from my life in Bangor, and what do you do? You go up there digging into my business, and for what? So you can run your mouth and tell everyone what a horrible person I am? You have no clue how horrible I can be, but tonight, I'm going to show you!"

Sarah screamed when Abby took a thick bladed knife from the nearby table and waved it toward her, "No! Abby! Please! Stop this!"

Abby sat the knife down and landed another blow across Sarah's face, "I told you to shut the hell up!"

More tears flew from Sarah's eyes as she tried to wiggle away and managed to topple her chair to the floor. The world turned sideways and blurred as Sarah hit her already injured head once more. The linoleum scuffed the side of her face with its waxy texture as she struggled not to lose consciousness. Sarah moaned as Abby grabbed the chair and slung it upright, the dizziness from her concussion making her nauseous.

Two folded pieces of paper had fallen from Sarah's back pocket on her way down to the floor. Abby snatched them up and looked at them, her eyes fixated. She read the words on the pages in shock and proceeded to wave the sheets in Sarah's face, "What is this? Where did you get this? How the hell...? No! There's no way! How in the hell are you making me dream of this?" Abby's voice cracked once again, her words barely understandable, "Where is this place?"

Sarah was afraid to speak, but managed a slight whisper, "The location is circled on the second page."

Abby howled in disbelief, "How are you in my dreams? Answer me!"

Sarah whimpered, "I don't know. I've dreamt of that place too."

The papers in Abby's hand crinkled under her grip as her fingers turned into tight knots. She tossed the sheets to the floor and reached for the knife. The strident scream that left her lungs was indistinguishable from the demonic apparition she resembled. She sprinted toward Sarah at full speed and landed the knife square into the left side of her chest.

∞

The sky above Sarah warped and spun as she tried to walk through the now familiar surroundings of Mystery Hill. The fog had been replaced by rain that poured down in heavy sheets. The falling liquid pressed her body closer toward the ground with each step forward. She fought frantically against the wet weight as it slowly pushed her to her knees. A spasm quivered across her back and into her extremities, her ability to move all but gone.

Sarah lay on the waterlogged ground, her face buried in thick mud as she tried desperately to breathe. She strained to kick her legs, but they would not respond. She was completely paralyzed; even her ability to scream had left her body.

The sound of the rain eventually cleared from Sarah's ears, and her sight blurred until it dissolved into oblivion. Everything that surrounded her faded away into the darkness, never to return.

CHAPTER FOURTEEN

Monday, September 22, 2014
Autumn Equinox...

The room was silent around Abby as she lay in the floor, her cheek against the clammy linoleum. The only sound she heard was the drumming of her own heartbeat. She pulled her legs toward her body and rhythmically rocked back and forth to the cadence of her heartbeat.

Abby wanted to run, to hide away and never see another person again, but she knew that there were things to do, and they needed to be done right now if she wanted to ensure her future with Thom. She rolled over and snapped to her feet. Sarah's body lay in the floor, still strapped to the wooden chair.

Abby walked around her body several times, as if she were studying Sarah's corpse for an autopsy. She leaned over the body and examined her face, her cheeks covered in dried tears. Abby's eyes worked their way downward until they stopped on the handle of the large knife that protruded from her chest, then continued to the blood pooled on the floor underneath.

Abby grabbed the handle and pulled it from Sarah's torso. She studied the blood as it coursed down the blade like rain rolling along the edge of a piece of glass, only thicker. She took the knife and made quick work of the cords that kept Sarah to the chair, her body rolled to rest on its front with the cut of the last binding.

Abby stared indifferently down at her back. She felt no remorse, no regret, and no sorrow for the girl that lay on the apartment floor. Sarah was nothing more than an obstacle that needed to be dealt with ruthlessly and efficiently. She stepped to the kitchen and searched for a box of trash bags in Sarah's cabinets. She grabbed a handful, returned to the body, and stood up the chair that lay on its side in the floor.

Abby shook one of the bags in the air until it opened, and slid the opening over

Sarah's feet. She pulled hard until the top of the bag reached Sarah's waist. She shook another bag in the air and slid it over Sarah's head in the same fashion. The third bag, she tore at its seam and laid it perpendicular to Sarah's body. She rolled the girl onto the bag's edge and wrapped her mid-section into the sheet of plastic and tied the pull strings from the other two bags together, to hold the third bag in place. She had been very careful not to let the trash bags touch the puddle of blood that had pooled in the floor; a problem she would have to deal with later.

Abby found Sarah's keys lying in one corner of the room and slid them in her pocket. She opened the front door and looked out into the darkness. No one was around. With a deep intake with her lungs, she hoisted the body over one shoulder, and made her way to Sarah's car.

With her free hand, Abby dug the keys from her pocket and hit a button on the key ring's fob, the trunk released with a slight click. She lowered her load into the opening and closed the trunk as quietly as she could manage.

Abby made her way back to the apartment and locked the door before returning to the car and sliding into the driver's seat. With a turn of the key, the engine roared to life and she backed out of the parking lot. It was time to take care of the contents of the trunk.

∞

Thom slowly parked his car in front of Sarah's apartment. It had been a long time since he had visited her place. It was something he was not looking forward to doing. But he hadn't been able to track down Abby, and he was worried about Sarah so he took a deep breath, stepped from his car and approached her door.

The sun's rays could be seen on the horizon as Thom pressed the doorbell on the doorframe. He tapped his foot impatiently as he waited for a reply. He rang again. Still nothing.

Thom stepped from the door and looked around to the parking lot. Sarah's car was nowhere in sight. That lightened his concern a bit. If Abby had shown up at her apartment, Sarah probably wasn't home. Instead of ringing the doorbell, he knocked loudly. Still no reply.

Thom sighed and returned to his car. He maneuvered his car from the parking lot somewhat disappointed, but relieved at the same time. Had Sarah answered the door, he hadn't been sure what he would have said to her. Still, it was worth coming back later in the day to speak with her about what had happened at his apartment.

As Thom made his way home, he decided it would be a good idea to make another quick pass by Abby's, just to see if her car was there. It was on the way to his apartment anyway, so it wasn't out of the way.

His car slid quietly into Abby's apartment complex and he passed by her building. Thom stopped in front of her door and scratched at his chin. Her car wasn't in its normal parking space. He made one loop around the lot and discovered she wasn't home either.

Thom pointed his car toward home and he couldn't help but think that something was seriously amiss with both girls not being home so early in the morning. A large yawn trumpeted from his mouth as he tried to keep his eyes on the road. Whatever was going on, it would have to wait until he had gotten a few hours' sleep.

∞

Abby could barely keep her eyes open as she drove down the long, country road. She had rolled both her windows down in hopes the cold air jetting into the car would keep her awake. It was several hours to the hog farm, and she was running on very little sleep. She slapped herself in the face a couple of times as she tried to jolt herself awake. With a flip of the radio's knob, she turned it to full volume, in hopes the blaring music would keep her from falling asleep.

By this point, the sun had made its way into the sky, its light poking at Abby's tired eyes, "It's not much farther," she mumbled to herself.

Abby felt the numbness of sleep overtaking her body when a familiar turnoff caught her attention. Her eyes widened and she whipped Sarah's car onto the single-lane dirt road. Memories of over a decade ago infiltrated her mind as she landed the car next to an old, metal fence. She could hear the familiar squeal of the animals on the other side when she turned off the car's motor.

Abby quickly reached down and flipped the trunk release; she saw the lid pop up in her rearview mirror as she stepped from the car. She made her way around to the hatch and reached down with aching arms. The black bags seemed to have grown considerably heavier than they were a few hours ago. She mustered what strength she had left and heaved Sarah's body from the trunk onto the ground. With both hands, she dragged the body to the edge of fence. Thoughts of her brother engulfed her. Abby wished he was there to help, even if she had to listen to his critical, self-righteous mutterings for another ten years.

The pigs on the other side of the fence pressed their bodies violently against the crisscrossed metal, their impatience showing in the growing volume and tempo of their squeals.

Abby pushed the bag on the side of the fence, the hogs pulling at the black wrapping with their muddy snouts. With one final lift, the bag flipped over the edge of the metal barrier and on top of the waiting animals.

The pigs twisted and flopped as they tried to move away, only to return to cover the bag with their filth coated bodies. She turned away and jumped into the car, fleeing from the sound of the pigs' grisly repast.

Without even closing the car's trunk, Abby turned the key and pressed the accelerator to the floorboard. Tears filled her eyes even though her emotions were disconnected and numb. The squealing of the hogs continued its reiteration inside her mind and her ears as she wiped away a tear, and sped back to Sarah's apartment.

CHAPTER FIFTEEN

After some much needed sleep, Thom locked up his apartment and got into his car. He gently rubbed his eyes when the afternoon sun reflected off the windshield. His first stop was Abby's, to see if she had returned home. A quick circle through her parking lot confirmed she still had not returned. It wasn't uncommon for her to stay at a friend's house watching movies into the wee hours of the morning, but to be gone this long wasn't her norm. Perhaps she was at work.

Thom punched in Abby's work number on his phone and waited for an answer. It wasn't Abby that greeted him, but one of the managers, "I don't know where she is. She should have been here an hour ago, and she hasn't called the store to say she wasn't coming into work."

Thom thanked the man and told him he'd make sure she called the store as soon as possible. He pressed on to Sarah's apartment, his worry mounting with each mile his car traveled.

Thom pulled into Sunset Ridge Apartments and immediately spied Sarah's car parked near her front door. A relieved sigh came from his lips as he parked next to her car. It was parked at an awkward angle; a third of her car took up the slot next to it. He stepped out of his car and walked over to Sarah's. If her parking job had not gotten his attention, the mud that caked the sides of her tires and covered the inside of her wheel wells certainly did.

Thom approached Sarah's door and started to press the doorbell, but suddenly thought better of it. He took ahold of the doorknob and gave it a slow, steady turn and carefully pushed the door open just enough to see inside the room. Through the small crack, he could see someone on their hands and knees, their back toward him, as they scrubbed feverishly at the floor.

Thom assumed it was Sarah and pushed the door wide. He took a few steps inside the room and closed the door. The girl's attention quickly went to him, her ginger ringlets hung limply down her shoulders, saturated in sweat.

Thom jumped back, "Abby! What the hell are you doing here?"

Abby slowly rose to her feet; red stains covered the knees of her jeans. She smiled sweetly at Thom and motioned him to come toward her. He didn't move an inch.

"Honey, could you help me clean up this stain. I don't want anyone to see it. I...I've tried so hard to get it out of the edge of the carpet...but I..."

Thom felt his body go numb as he took in the scene. There was blood smeared on the linoleum, and the carpet had a smaller, dark stain which had soaked deep into its fibers. Abby's pants were covered in more blood, as well as the cleaning gloves and pink-tinted sponge she gripped in one hand.

Abby broke down at that point; she dropped the sponge and threw her face into her bloody hands, "I need your help, Thom! I can't let Sarah see this mess!"

Thom took a step backward as he blindly reached for the doorknob. His hand missed its mark, so he turned his head to grab the knob, and a scream shot from Abby, "Where are you going, Thom? You can't leave me now! I need you to help me!"

Abby lunged for a blood soaked knife that rested on the coffee table. Thom grabbed her by one wrist and pulled her toward him. The knife slipped to the floor, Abby still trying to get her free hand on its handle.

Abby howled as Thom held her arm tightly, "Let go of me!"

Thom managed to pull the writhing girl close enough to him to grab her other arm and flung her toward the door to keep her away from the knife.

Abby righted herself and launched toward Thom's ankles. He fell to the floor, but quickly rolled himself in the direction of the door. She managed to pluck the knife from the floor just as Thom opened the door and made for his car. Abby chased after him, knife still in hand.

Thom dug into his pocket for his car keys, and jabbed them into the lock. He propelled his body over the driver's seat and grabbed the black bag resting on the passenger side of the car. He had just enough time to unzip the bag on the seat and remove his pistol before Abby rounded the car door with her knife.

"Back off, Abby!"

She froze in her tracks as she stared at the barrel of the 9mm pistol.

Thom slid himself across his seat until he could stand; Abby slowly moved backward as he inched away from his car door.

She continued to back away until she was beside Sarah's car. Before Thom could react, Abby popped open the car door and jumped inside. The car roared to life. She threw the car in gear and Thom launched himself back into his car, Abby missing him by inches before she took off out of the parking lot.

Thom rose up and saw Abby speed away. He jumped from his seat and ran inside Sarah's apartment, "Sarah? Sarah, where are you?" He searched her entire apartment, but she was nowhere inside.

He looked at the blood stains on the floor, and emotion finally overtook his body. Thom cried out in sorrow at the thought of what Abby had done to Sarah.

Thom rubbed his eyes and realized there was blood all over his hands from his struggle with Abby. The sight brought more tears and he ran to the kitchen sink to wash the stains from his hands. Thom scrubbed vigorously until all the crimson had been completely removed from his fingers and palms. He then wiped a rag viciously across his face until the red tinge dissipated from his lids.

Thom reached for a towel and noticed a single sheet of paper next to the sink, a bloody handprint on one side. The picture on the paper nearly sent Thom to his knees. It was the stone circle from his nightmares. He read the page over and over again as he staggered out of the apartment completely dazed from shock. He fell into the driver's seat of his car as he stared blankly at the name above the photo, *Mystery Hill*.

The entire story was not contained on the piece of paper, but there was enough to deduce where Abby was headed. Thom reached for his cellphone and activated his GPS. He typed feverishly on its small keyboard the words 'Mystery Hill' and within seconds, the device beeped a match to his inquiry.

Thom attached his phone to the dash as it began to speak its instructions, "*You will reach Mystery Hill in approximately forty-six minutes.*"

∞

Abby studied the sheet of paper once more to make sure she was following the directions she had scribbled down earlier. Mystery Hill wasn't far away and, in her mind at least, the stone circle was the only safe place for her to go. Thom had seen what she had done in Sarah's apartment. Perhaps the place she kept visiting in her dreams could somehow make her safe again.

A sign on the side of the road confirmed she was headed the right direction.

Mystery Hill 2 Miles

Abby had discarded the bloody gloves she had been wearing, but she still had her knife resting in the seat next to her. She was going to make sure she received the help she wanted, even if it took some coercion to get that assistance. What other choice did she have?

Abby took in a long breath, and let it out in short bursts as she turned the car onto the drive that led to Mystery Hill. As the sun slowly sank behind the trees in front of her, she could make out the shape of a building in the distance. She drove up to the porch and shoved the car into park. To her surprise, a long haired Native American man stepped from the building and waved in her direction.

She stepped from the car and the man on the porch froze, his smile faded away as he took in her condition, "Young lady, can I help you?"

Abby pointed her knife at the stranger and stepped forward, her stride was unbalanced and shaky as she advanced. She waved a sheet of paper at him, "Yes, you *can* help me. You can tell me why I dream of this place, almost every night. I'm haunted by this place! Please, help me!"

The man stood firm in his place, "If you want my help, you will put down that knife. Otherwise, I guess you will have to use it, if you think you can."

Abby looked at the knife in her hand and slowly sat it on the ground.

"Please step away from it," he requested.

She took several steps toward the porch; the look on the man's face was one of concern, not fear.

He crossed his hands across his chest, "There. Now, perhaps we can talk. By the looks of you, I'd say you've had more than bad dreams haunting you. Would you like to tell me what happened?"

Abby wildly shook her head, "No! I'll not tell you anything!"

He stiffened and cleared his throat, "If you want my help, I would suggest you drop the attitude."

She thought about retrieving her knife, but thought better of it as she watched the man's expression. She knew if she tried anything, it would not go well for her. She walked to the porch, sat on the bottom step and began to sob furiously.

The man took a few steps and settled himself next to her. "My name is Richard Adahy. I am the caretaker of Mystery Hill."

She managed to say her name between sobs, "Abby Morris."

"So, Miss Morris, tell me what has happened.

Abby mustered up what little energy she had left and poured out her soul to Richard. She told him about what happened to Jennifer Kelly over a decade ago. She explained the years of rumors and paranoia as she tried to conceal the insanity that hid just under the surface, and how she eventually left her hometown of Bangor and moved to Manchester. Abby also described how she and Thom first met, how his ex-girlfriend kept getting in the way, and how the ex had traveled to Maine to dig into Abby's past; she also told of all the dreams she'd had about Mystery Hill. Finally, Abby got into what had transpired over the last few hours.

Richard took in her words as she laid it all out to him, every small detail. Once Abby had finished, he then looked at his watch and rose to his feet as he debated his options. He looked down at Abby and met her eyes, "I may be able to help you."

Richard took a long breath and went into detail about how the stone circle at Mystery Hill functioned as a time gate, and worked around the spring and fall equinoxes. Abby listened with intrigue as she learned it was possible for her to travel back in time. The Indian added a warning at the end of his story, "Abby, I want you to understand something. I'm not sure you are meant to travel within the circle. This journey may ultimately kill you."

Abby looked up and met Richard's eyes, "What other choice do I have?"

Richard shook his head and didn't reply. He only looked at his watch again and sighed, "If we are going to do this, we have to do it now."

Abby nodded and rose to her feet as her body shook with fatigue, "Tell me what I have to do."

CHAPTER SIXTEEN

Richard led Abby to the top of Mystery Hill. Without his companion, Percy, perched on his shoulder, he was very apprehensive as he prepared Abby for her journey through the void. He looked the young lady over; the dried blood still covered the knees of her jeans. Richard tried his best to ignore it. There was no time. "First, I need you to kneel here," he pointed to the heart of the circle.

Abby hesitated for a moment, but finally complied.

"Now, when in the past do you want to arrive?"

Abby thought hard, "July fourth of two thousand three."

Richard thought for a moment, "I can't send you back to that exact date. It will have to be September the twenty-third of the previous year."

Abby started to protest, but Richard cut her off, "That is the closest that I can send you to the date you have requested."

She frowned at Richard but said nothing.

"Once you have completed whatever you plan to do in the past, I will need you to return to Mystery Hill so that I can bring you back to your own time."

Abby nodded in response.

"I need you to concentrate on the date that I told you, September the twenty-third, two thousand two. Otherwise you could be lost in the void which separates this point in time with the one you are about to visit. If that happens, you will be left floating in an endless moment of time, existing in the heart of nothingness forever."

Abby mumbled under her breath, "I understand."

Richard stepped in front of Abby and looked down into her strained face, "I will be there when you arrive in the past to help you on your way. Now, I need you to close your eyes, and concentrate on my voice."

Abby complied.

Richard placed his hands on Abby's head, "Now, I need you to completely clear your mind. Think of nothing but the date of September the twenty-third, two thousand two. Keep your eyes closed and concentrate."

∞

Abby had no desire to live in the past for nearly ten months. Instead of following his direction, she concentrated on July the fourth, two thousand three.

Her lids closed tightly, she repeated her date endlessly in her head, "

"July the fourth, two thousand three. July the fourth, two thousand three."

Abby could feel the breeze around her as it blew her hair slightly to the right. She could hear Richard begin to chant in an unknown language, his voice barely audible over the increasing winds.

Richard's hands left her head, and she sensed him step away. The air's motion amplified, making it impossible to hear Richard's unknown words. The howl of the wind even extended to her thoughts. As the air around her roared, she felt the ground underneath her begin to soften, as if it were fading away. She felt herself become weightless, her body floating with nothing above or below it.

Abby kept her eyes closed, her heart racing with excitement, "July the fourth, two thousand three," she yelled in her mind.

Abby wanted to open her eyes, to see the void that Richard had spoken of, but she did not. She continued to repeat the date she had imprinted into her brain. Pain licked at her limbs as she fell through the void, and she could hear faint whispers as her body twisted end over end.

Without warning, her body crashed into cold stone which knocked the breath from her lungs. She wheezed and sputtered in agony, her eyes still tightly closed. Abby took in several long drags of air as she tried to replace what had been knocked from her body. The wind that had whipped in her ears slowly began to fade. She popped open her eyes and the air stopped all together.

Abby slowly rose to her feet and looked for Richard. He was nowhere to be found. A shot of fear shook Abby's core as she whispered to the night sky, "Richard said he would be here to help me."

∞

Thom had followed his GPS' direction step by step as the sun's light slowly faded into the trees around him. His heart began to race as he neared his destination. Night after night, his dreams had taken him to this place called Mystery Hill. He felt an ill-placed nostalgia as he turned his car up the drive and saw the building that rested against the trees. His mind raced in anticipation of what he would find when he arrived.

Thom parked his car next to Sarah's and his heart sank as he pondered what Abby might have done to the girl, but his suspicions had been correct. Abby had come here.

He reached over to his passenger seat and grasped the pistol in one hand before exiting his car. He cautiously stepped to the porch and looked through the glass and saw what appeared to be an office. A quick tug at the door told him it was locked.

Thom scanned his surroundings and looked down at his watch; within a few minutes it would be dark. He spied a trail that led away from the office building and quickly took to it. He could see that it led up the side of the hill, but it wasn't just because he could see that the path wormed its way upward, it was because he had been here in his dreams, more times than he could possibly count.

Thom could feel his emotions ignite like a fuel soaked wick as he reached the top of the trail and looked ahead. The wind around him stung at his skin as he continued forward. He could hear someone's voice ahead of him, at what appeared to be the center of a swirling vortex of air. He lowered his body nearer the ground and advanced, tenaciously determined to get to the center of what lay ahead of him.

Thom shielded his eyes as the wind grew stronger with each step he took. The wind howled in his ears to the point he could hear nothing but the roar of white noise. Sweat poured from his face as he fought against the constant gust of air. Leaves and debris caught in the whirlwind pelted into his body as he continued to advance.

Thom could see a man standing at one end of the large stone circle. He chanted in a language Thom had not heard before. At the epicenter of the circle and cyclone knelt Abby, her chin held high and her eyes closed.

Thom watched in awe as Abby's form gradually dissolved into the air, like a tall pile of leaves dispersing on the wind. Then, just as suddenly as it had started, the air around him stilled, and an eerie silence fell over the forest.

The air that had resisted Thom vanished away and he pitched forward to the ground. He quickly jumped to his feet, his pistol still held tightly in his clinched hand. He marched toward the stranger as he tried to catch his breath. The man in front of Thom spun around, his eyes filled with surprise at his presence.

Thom had his gun at the ready, his breath labored from falling to the ground with such force, "What...what did you do to her?"

The man held up a hand and spoke softly, "Nothing that she didn't wish to happen."

Without warning, an unearthly screech reverberated around Thom, its sound echoing off the large stones around him. Out of the sky flew the creature of his nightmares; the winged animal barreled directly toward where he stood.

Thom panicked and squeezed the trigger on the pistol, but the crow simply faded away in the air. Next, the man in front of him disappeared in front of his eyes. Then everything around him went black. Thom's entire existence vanished into nothing, until even he faded into the unknown.

CHAPTER SEVENTEEN

Friday, July 4, 2003...

Abby's legs quivered underneath her own weight as she tried to step forward and felt her muscles give way to gravity. She fell to the ground and convulsed uncontrollably at the center of the stone circle. Desperation flooded her mind as she tried to lock her eyes on any fixed object near her. Her arms and legs quaked with one spasm after the next, the cold stones against her body her only companions.

It felt like an eternity had passed before the trembling throughout her body finally ceased. She rolled onto her back and stared into the night sky. The air was warm on her skin as she finally regained the ability to focus on her surroundings.

Abby stayed on her back for several minutes as she rested her body that was wracked with stinging pain. She looked at her arms to discover they had been cut open in several places. Long scratches covered her limbs, like someone had taken a steel comb and ran it along the surface of her flesh. She examined the cuts closely and saw they were not bleeding, but only raw to the touch.

Abby carefully pushed herself to a sitting position and tried to see into the night. The moon above her cast just enough light for her to see the path at the edge of the stone circle.

With as much effort as she could gather, Abby pushed herself to her feet. Her body ached with each step as she worked her way to the start of the path. She warily progressed down the side of Mystery Hill until the ground leveled and she could see Richard's office.

A car sat in front of the building, and she could hear voices from the front door as she stepped onto the porch. Abby felt into her back pocket, relieved to find the knife she had plucked from the ground when Richard wasn't looking. She cautiously peered inside the office and found a young man sitting in front of a large desk, and another man that looked much like Richard, only decades older. Perhaps it was his father, Abby presumed.

The two men carried on in their conversation and Abby sprang into action. She pulled the knife from her back pocket and charged into the room. She jumped behind the young fellow and placed the knife to his throat. The old Indian scowled at her as he studied her every move, "I promise you, there is no need for that," he rumbled.

Abby's voice was sharp and direct, "I want the keys to the car outside! Now!"

The young man slowly reached to his side and unlatched the clip that held his keys to his belt loop. He nervously raised the keys with one hand, "Here, take it," he quivered.

Abby snatched the keys and bolted out the door only to be smacked in the face by a dark mass of feathers. The creature squawked with rage as Abby ducked low to prevent another attack. She managed her way to the side of the car, opened the door just enough to squeeze herself in, and slammed it shut.

The crow launched itself at the windshield; its talons gripped ahold of one of the car's wipers and ripped it away.

Abby started the car and floored the gas pedal, the crow still hot on her trail as she sped up the driveway. She pulled onto the main road, her eyes glued to the rearview mirror of her stolen car. The crow had vanished from sight as quickly as it had arrived.

She clicked on the radio, in hopes it would calm her nerves, but the music gave her little comfort as she made her way toward Maine.

∞

Four hours later...

Abby hummed slightly to herself as she neared the town of Hampden. It brought an odd calmness to see the city over ten years younger. The radio had confirmed the date; it was the Fourth of July, two thousand three. She felt an optimistic smugness that she had arrived on the date she had wanted, rather than listening to Richard's directions and arriving ten months earlier. Maybe it was a good omen.

Abby circled through the town a few times and relived memories of being seventeen years old. The pressure of what had happened with Jennifer Kelly did not exist, because it had yet to happen. However, as the evening grew later, she knew it was time to make her way to the house of her old high school crush, Matt.

Abby located Elm Street and drove slowly along its sidewalked roadways, and took in its familiar scenery. She loved this section of town. As a teen, it always filled her heart with joy to drive down its lighted streets. But most of all, it was where Matt lived.

She found his house with her memory as her guide, and parked just across the street. She could see that several cars were already sitting at his place; that told her the party had already started. Music could be heard as it echoed across the road and Abby closed her eyes. She listened with wistfulness to the sounds of more than a decade ago.

A pair of headlights made their way up the street. That snapped Abby back into reality. The car slowed, and then stopped in the driveway beside Matt's house. She smiled at the vehicle she recognized all too well. It was her old car from high school, a two thousand one, red Dodge Neon.

Abby quickly jumped from her car and made her way across the road. She watched as her younger self stepped from the Neon and started for Matt's door. She called to her younger self, "Abby!"

The younger, beautifully dressed version of herself turned and gasped, "Oh my God! What happened to you?"

Abby looked down at herself and realized she was still covered in Sarah's dried blood.

The younger Abby looked at her closer, and older Abby could see on her face as she connected the dots that they were both the same person.

Older Abby stepped closer, "Please, don't go in there. Stay away from that party.

Tonight will be the worst night of your life if you don't listen to me."

Younger Abby screamed at the top of her lungs and darted toward Matt's door. Older Abby took after her, and dived for her ankles, which sent the young woman to the ground.

The older girl held on as tight as she could, and worked her way up the younger girl's body. Younger Abby fought and kicked but couldn't break the grasp the older girl had on her body.

Older Abby tried to cover her mouth to prevent the sound of her screams from reaching the ears of the partygoers inside the house. Her only hope was the deafening music would muffle the ruckus outside. Younger Abby bit into her hand and caused the older girl to shriek in pain, "Listen to me! If you go in there, people will die!"

Younger Abby ignored her plea and continued to fight.

Tears began to pour from the older girl's eyes, her mental anguish reaching an exhausted plateau as she reached into her back pocket and retrieved the knife she had stashed there earlier. It was time to win this fight, but it meant the unthinkable.

Abby held the knife to the young girl's throat, tears falling onto her like rain, "Abby, I...I'm so sorry. I don't know what else to do. No one else can die because of us. I have to fix this."

With one swift stroke, Abby ran the blade across the neck of her younger self. The girl's body went rigid in shock and collapsed into the grass around them.

Older Abby stood as she sobbed; her tears were too many to see the body that laid motionless in the dark.

Abby wiped her eyes just in time to see the front door to the house open, and Matt step onto the porch. She smiled at his handsomeness and turned her face up toward the sky. Above her, the black shape of a crow circled around her once and landed gracefully on her shoulder. Her body became surrounded by a blinding, white light, and she faded from existence.

EPILOGUE

Saturday, August 30, 2014...

Richard stood at the edge of Hampton Beach, Percy perched on his shoulder. The two watched a group of thirty or so people as they stood in the sand, a warm breeze blowing off the Atlantic.

In the distance, Richard could see a lady in an exquisite, flowing gown, and a man in a white tuxedo. A smile crossed over his lips as the couple took one another's hands. The minister next to them inhaled deeply and beamed before he spoke.

Only Richard and Percy knew of the sacrifice that Abby Morris had made, however selfish her motivations might have been. She had taken her own life and because of that, other lives would continue.

She had saved the lives of two people, and the integrity of another.

Richard gave his winged companion a rub on the head, "At least we know."

Percy blinked his black eyelids and bobbed his head in agreement. The crow's disappearance had not been an accident. It had been a necessary trial to prove Richard's worth. Even without Percy at his side, he had the strength within himself to select the best choices when it involved the use of Mystery Hill's power. When Percy returned to the stone circle, he had also brought the knowledge of Abby's sacrifice to his Indian companion. The two shared a bond that transcended mankind's understanding of the universe.

Richard and Percy inched closer to the ceremony, but not close enough to draw any unwanted attention. They could see Thomas Collier as he grinned with celestial delight, a sight Richard rarely got to witness. The young man seemed to glow as he looked into his bride-to-be's eyes, emotion about to burst from his very soul.

Sarah Wisdom mirrored Thom's luminous look, her cheeks radiating with excitement. Her alluring brunette locks rolled down from under her white veil.

The two repeated the minister's words and then Thom pulled a slip of paper from inside his jacket. He looked to the crowd and then to Sarah, his voice fluctuating with the nervousness that was visible in his trembling hands, "Ladies and gentlemen. I have something here that I wrote for my beautiful wife-to-be, and I want to read it before we share our first kiss as husband and wife.

Richard could see Sarah wipe away a tear of happiness as she stared into Thom's eyes.

Thom cleared his throat and began to read, *"The heart and the mind are the two components of every single being on this earth. Two separate pieces, rarely ever touching, but are well aware of each other's presence. They are the two strongest forces, forever fighting for dominance, with completely unique goals.*

But sometimes, the two are bridged by a force completely unseen by the naked eye, held together by a force so overwhelmingly strong, yet as weak as the breath of a whisper.

Your soul has become that bridge for me, Sarah, fortified by stone and held together by the trust which I hold in you, forever."

The crowd began to cheer as the minister looked to Thom, "You may kiss your bride."

ACKNOWLEDGEMENTS

One thing that I always enjoy about finishing a book is writing the acknowledgements. (I wonder if there is a misplaced career opportunity in simply writing acknowledgements? Ha!)

First, I have to thank everyone that has stuck with me as I continue to write my little tales. This story has been a long time coming, and is finally complete for your enjoyment. Your faith in my storytelling is a big part of what keeps me writing.

A special thanks to Melissa Haddock for her help in proofreading, editing, and just general brainstorming with this latest work. Her countless read-throughs ultimately helped this book make it into print. The time and effort she put into it were priceless!

Major appreciations go out to Jeff Quillen for letting me quote from his song *Hands of Time*. I've known Jeff for years, and he is a fine musician and song writer! Check out his current band's website at: http://www.jeffquillenband.com

Also, thank you to Stephanie White for her stunning cover art. She never disappoints in the quality of her craft. Anyone reading this should take a moment and view her work at the website listed below: http://www.stephscoverdesign.com

Finally, and most importantly, I thank our Heavenly Father. If it were not for Him looking out for me, I could not write these books for people to enjoy!

The Fear Series

By L R Barrett-Durham and E G Glover

Available on Kindle and paperback from Van Pelt Press

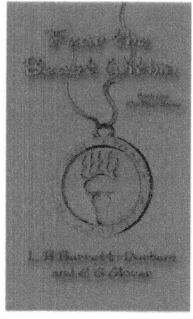

"This first book in the "Fear"
series will keep you on the edge of your
seat."

"Very unpredictable, exciting, nail biting,
and pretty steamy at times."

"From the first page it sucks you right in
and you literally do not want to put it down!"

"Excellent!....Mind blowing!....."

"I absolutely LOVED the first book of the
series, Fear the Beast Within, and didn't
think it could get any better, but I was SO
WRONG!!!!"

"Grady and Leia have done it again!"

"This book was great! They really knocked it
out of the park with this one!"

"The writers know how to keep you on the
edge of your seat the whole time.

"The third book of the series and it's
definitely a winner!!!!"

~Reviews from Amazon.com

MYSTERY HILL SERIES

BOOK ONE: A TWIST IN TIME

BY E G GLOVER

AVAILABLE ON KINDLE AND PAPERBACK FROM
RELATIVE TERM PRESS

"Great story about a love that never dies."

"This is an absolute great read!! Loved it very much. It gives us a glimpse into such a great love that transcends time."

"The characters were well-developed and believable."

~Reviews from Amazon.com

ABOUT THE AUTHOR

E G Glover lives in northwest Alabama, with his wife, two daughters, and their many purr-babies. After being diagnosed with multiple sclerosis in 2010, he has taken on writing as a full time venture. Along with *The Mystery Hill Series*, he is also co-writer on the paranormal romance stories of *The Fear Series*.

He is a collector of retro electronics and a lover of the science fiction realm, *Doctor Who* being his favorite piece of work in that genre.

You can find E G Glover at:
http://egglover.wix.com/books
OR
http://www.facebook.com/EGGlover1976

www.ingramcontent.com/pod-product-compliance
Lightning Source LLC
Chambersburg PA
CBHW020245150626
46552CB00020B/227